DEKOK AND
THE DISILLUSIONED CORPSE

DeKok
and the
Disillusioned Corpse

by

BAANTJER

translated from the Dutch by H.G. Smittenaar

INTERCONTINENTAL PUBLISHING

ISBN 1 881164 06 3

Printing History:
  1st Dutch printing: 1977
  2nd Dutch printing: 1978
  3rd Dutch printing: 1980
  4th Dutch printing: 1983
  5th Dutch printing: 1985
  6th Dutch printing: 1987
  7th Dutch printing: 1988
  8th Dutch printing: 1988
  9th Dutch printing: 1988
  10th Dutch printing: 1989
  11th Dutch printing: 1990
  12th Dutch printing: 1991
  13th Dutch printing: 1992
  14th Dutch printing: 1993

  1st American edition: 1993

A condensed version of this book appeared in the original language in *Het Beste
boek*, (Best Books) a publication of Uitgeversmaatschappij The Reader's Digest. ©
1985 by Uitgeversmaatschappij The Reader's Digest N.V., Amsterdam & Brussels.

Cover drawing by: Judy Sardella
Typography: Monica S. Rozier
Manufactured by BookCrafters, Inc., Fredericksburg, VA

DeKok
and the
Disillusioned Corpse

1

It was only March, but it was warm for the time of year. A mild spring sun peeked through the budding elms at the edge of the Brewers Canal in Amsterdam and darted playfully across the surface of the water. Detective-Inspector DeKok of the Warmoes Street Station stood on the aft deck of a flat coal barge and observed two dispassionate men from the special Drown Unit of the Municipal Medical Service. The men were in the process of fishing a male corpse from the murky waters of the canal. Carefully they pulled the corpse higher, but they could not prevent it scraping against the brick sides of the canal.

The Inspector wiped the sweat off his brow with the back of his hand. When the call first came in, he decided to walk to the scene. It was not all that far from the station house and he preferred walking anyway. It was a nice day and a corpse would not run away. But young Vledder, his friend, assistant, colleague and partner had not been able to match the older man's sedate walking pace. In his youthful enthusiasm he had increased the tempo considerably.

DeKok was still trying to catch his breath. The hand-knitted sweater that his caring wife nagged him into wearing when there was still an "r" in the month was uncomfortably warm underneath his jacket. He pushed his little, decrepit felt hat further back on his head and loosened his tie.

The Paramedics pulled the net onto dry land and prepared to place the corpse on the stretcher. It was all routine. They did not get excited. One more drowning was nothing to be concerned about. In a country where everybody had to learn to swim in grade school, it was surprising that so many people still drowned in the many canals of Amsterdam. Idly DeKok thought about the fact that Amsterdam had more canals and bridges than Venice. Vledder had once told him that and when he had not believed it, the young man had provided incontrovertible proof.

DeKok jumped from the coal barge onto the shore and in his typical, somewhat waddling gait moved toward the activity around the corpse. Together with Vledder he leaned forward and looked at the body. The canal water stank.

The dead man was a tall, slender, well-built man, still relatively young. DeKok estimated his age at thirty, perhaps thirty-five years. Certainly not older. He was wearing black jeans and a dark-blue turtle-neck sweater. Nothing else. No jacket, no overcoat. The proportionally somewhat small feet were shod with new Keds. The hair that partly obscured his face with disordered, wet strands was thin, straight and ash-blond.

With a thick forefinger DeKok pushed the eyelids open one by one. The irises were light blue and the pupils were normal, neither narrowed, nor abnormally widened. The face offered no particulars. It was oval with sunken cheeks. The rough skin with deep pores was slightly tanned. He had a sharp, almost pointy nose and a broad, firm chin. Strong, regular, white teeth could be glimpsed in the half-open mouth. According to the usual ways in which such things are measured, the dead man had a handsome face with a friendly, open expression.

The death mask was flawed by a large, gaping wound that started just above the left eye and ran diagonally into the hairline for another inch or so. There was no jewelry on the long, strong fingers. There were no indications of a previously worn wedding ring.

Vledder looked a question at DeKok.

"Post mortem?"

"You mean the wound?"

"Looks nasty, don't you think?"

DeKok nodded slowly.

"It's a serious wound all right. But it doesn't have to mean anything. It's entirely possible that the man walked into the canal by accident and then drowned. The head wound could have happened after his death ... what do you call that again?"

"Post mortem."

DeKok coughed.

"Right ... it could have happened post-mortem. For instance, he could have been hit by the screw of an excursion boat, or something like that."

Vledder looked at his older colleague from aside. The mocking "post mortem" had not escaped him.

"No excursion boats go through the Brewers Canal," he replied sharply.

DeKok smiled.

"Very good," he said, admiration in his voice. "But you forget that the water in the canals is drained into the sea via the North Sea Canal. At night there's quite a current in the canals."

Vledder nodded his understanding.

"You mean to say the man didn't *have* to wind up in the water around here."

"That's it. Corpses can travel considerable distances in our canal system. I could tell you stories . . ." DeKok grimaced. "You can never predict where they'll wind up."

Vledder chewed his lower lip while he thought. He was not from Amsterdam originally and was always amazed when he learned something else about his adopted city. He knew, of course, that Amsterdam was completely below sea level. The canals were a left-over from the time that the city was both an important fort and a major harbor. The canals, in addition to promoting trade, also drained the water from the soggy bottom on which the city was built. But he had not known that the water was regularly replaced. Of course, the excess water had to go somewhere. He just had not thought about it.

After a while he gestured in the direction of the corpse.

"I don't know," he said with a slight hesitation, "but I have the feeling that he's going to cause a lot of trouble. Despite your theory about screws and all . . . I don't like that strange wound on his head. Besides, he doesn't look like the kind of man that just happens to walk into the water."

DeKok looked at him.

"What do you mean by *happen*?"

"I mean, without a push."

DeKok did not react. He was capable of ignoring things and people with supreme indifference when it suited him. Slowly he straightened out from his bent position and gestured toward the Paramedics. They picked up the stretcher and pushed it into the ambulance. Then they closed the doors. The small crowd of curious Amsterdammers evaporated.

The gray sleuth placed his hand on the muscular shoulder of his younger colleague.

"It's probably best," he said, "if you go with the ambulance. Have them take the body directly to the Pathology lab. I'll alert the fingerprint boys and the photographer. They'll meet you there. When they are finished, have the corpse stripped and send the clothes to Forensic. You never know. Make sure you have an accurate description and look for papers."

"Then what?"

"Then you're through for the time being. I'll inform the Commissaris* myself and will ask for Dr. Rusteloos to do an autopsy ... eh," he smiled, "I mean a post mortem."

"And where will I find you, afterward?"

DeKok grinned.

"If I'm not in the office ... I'll be at Little Lowee's. My parched throat cries out for the velvet touch of a smooth and venerable cognac."

* * *

Detective-Inspector DeKok hoisted his body onto a stool in front of the bar in the sparsely lit, intimate space that constituted the establishment of Little Lowee. After he was seated to his satisfaction, he looked around. He had a good view of the other customers from his accustomed place at the end of the bar, next to the wall, but the man he was looking for was not present.

He rested his forearms on the bar and waited for Little Lowee to perform his magic. He had informed his immediate superior, the Commissaris, who in the course of routine events had informed the Judge-Advocate and had

_____

* Commissaris = a rank equivalent to Captain.

11

passed on the request to Dr. Rusteloos to perform the autopsy at his earliest convenience. In his heart he hoped that the pathologist would discover a large amount of alcohol in the blood of the victim. In that case it could be safely assumed that the man had walked into the canal while under the influence of intoxicants. It would not be the first time that such a thing had happened. And if the good doctor then also would be obliging enough to declare that the head wound had happened *after* death by drowning, then the case would be finished as soon as Vledder had concocted the shortest of possible reports. DeKok would like that. He didn't really like puzzles. In his long career he had solved too many puzzles.

"If wishes were horses," thought DeKok, "all beggars would ride." He smiled to himself. His old mother had known thousands of sayings like that and DeKok remembered them all. But Vledder was right. The man did not look like the type that would stumble into a canal by accident.

He placed his little hat on his knees and leaned comfortably against the wall. He liked sitting here, at the end of the bar. Whenever possible he would stop by at Little Lowee's place. He had done that almost from the beginning of his police career. During good weeks he sometimes made it three or four times a week. Little Lowee's had almost become a necessity of life.

The small barkeeper approached him, wiping his hands on a towel.

"The same recipe?" he asked. It was almost always the same question, although he knew very well what DeKok drank.

Without waiting for an answer, Lowee grabbed a bottle of fine Napoleon cognac from under the counter. A bottle he kept especially for DeKok. With the same routine gesture

12

he placed two snifters next to the bottle and poured generous measures.

"You've been busy, I guess. Ain't seen you for a coupla days. I missed you," remarked Lowee conversationally.

DeKok grinned.

"And I missed my cognac."

He took the fragile glass into his big hand and rocked it slightly while he inhaled the stimulating aroma with a contended sigh. A look of happiness appeared on his melancholy face while he carefully took the first sip.

"You know, Lowee," he said, "I'd almost forgotten how it tasted."

The small barkeeper laughed. His friendly, mousy face became all wrinkles as he did so.

"I just got another case in," he said.

With a reverent gesture DeKok replaced his glass on the bar and leaned forward.

"Where can I find Slippery Eel?" he whispered.

Lowee's face fell. It assumed a martyr's look.

"You want 'im for something?"

DeKok smiled.

"Worried?"

The barkeeper shrugged his shoulders in a resigned movement.

"You gotta remember," he said sadly, "they're me customers. Iffen I gives them all to you, I might as well go outa business."

DeKok smiled.

"Doesn't he usually work alone?"

"Who?"

"Slippery."

"Yes."

"Still?"

A cunning look appeared on the narrow face of the barkeeper.

"Why you want to know?"

DeKok looked nonchalantly at nothing in particular.

"I thought he had a partner these days."

Lowee looked around him with a hunted look in his eyes. He was looking for eavesdroppers. Even in his own bar he was always cautious. He had been supplying DeKok with information for years, but nobody had ever been able to prove it. This was partly because of the type of information Lowee supplied and under what circumstances and partly because of what DeKok did with the information. For one thing, Lowee's information never showed up in any official reports. With the exception of Vledder, nobody on the force even knew that DeKok had this particular source.

Apparently satisfied that the coast was clear, Lowee leaned closer.

"Yes," he whispered, "he had a partner, but they broke up."

DeKok stared at him, willing him to continue.

"You knows that Slippery fell from a roof, last year, you know, during a breakie?"

DeKok nodded slowly.

"Yes. A villa at River Lane. He went from one hospital to another. It took him months to get over it. Still has some trouble with it."

Little Lowee looked sad.

"Yessir. Something with his back. It were because of the fall, I thinks. Some verte ... verte ... some bones in his backbone done slipped, or something. Anyways, they thought he'd have to live in a wheelchair the rest of his life. But they got him good enough that it weren't needed. They fixed him up good. Hardly can see a thing, anymore." The

14

barkeeper shook his head. "But Slippery weren't hisself no more after that. He don't move so fast no more, you see. It just don't work so good, no more. Also, he got scared."

DeKok grinned.

"That's why he sought a partner to take care of the dangerous stuff?"

Lowee raised one shoulder.

"You could say that." His voice was hesitant. "But you gotta see it from both sides. I mean, Slippery has a lotta smarts, you gotta give him that. He knows things. You cain't get that from the five-and-dime. That takes years. Believe you me, Slippery Eel knows what's what."

DeKok nodded agreement.

"Where did he find his sidekick?"

Lowee made a helpless gesture.

"I don't know. Nobody do. All at oncet, there he were. We just heard he and Slippery was partners."

"Why did they quarrel?"

The small barkeeper raised his hands in despair.

"You gotta ask the Eel yourself."

DeKok lifted his glass and laughed.

"Well, we're right back where we started. Where can I find Slippery Eel?"

Little Lowee sighed deeply.

"I'll tell him you wants to see him."

It did not sound wholehearted.

* * *

"And?"

Vledder pulled a doubtful face.

"Doesn't look too good. The man had nothing on him."

"Nothing?"

15

The young Inspector shook his head dejectedly.

"No papers, no money, nothing. Not even a single coin. He is not listed among Missing Persons. I checked that. Not even somebody who looks like him."

"What about the clothes?"

"Apparently all the numbers, marks, tags, what have you, have been removed. In some cases you could still see the holes where identifying marks had been cut out."

DeKok pushed his lower lip forward.

"Indeed? That's not so good. What did the finger boys have to say for themselves?"

"I asked them to correlate the information as soon as possible. They did. No match in their collection,."

DeKok rubbed a hand over his face.

"In other words ... we're stuck with an unidentified corpse."

Vledder sank down in his chair.

"That's not the worst. The man was murdered."

2

"Murdered?"

"Yes."

"Who was the coroner?"

"Old Doctor Koning. I had the impression that he was totally convinced. He said that he didn't want to anticipate the results of the post mor ... eh, the *autopsy*, but he was willing to go on record that the man had not died because of drowning."

DeKok pulled on his lower lip.

"Not by drowning," he said slowly.

Vledder shook his head.

"According to Doc Koning, the man was dead before he landed in the water."

DeKok nodded thoughtfully, his face serious.

"To tell you the truth, I was afraid of that. It just didn't look like an accident. Did you ask how the doctor arrived at his conclusion?"

Vledder smiled.

"Never had a chance. I was to ask Dr. Rusteloos tomorrow *after* the autopsy and he said that *he* would add his findings to those of the pathologist. Didn't believe in spreading pre-conceived ideas *before* an autopsy."

"Quite right," said the DeKok. "Then what?"

"Then he told me the man was dead."

"That's all?"

"Just about. Well, anyway, he did allow as how death had not occurred naturally and that perhaps it could be termed a violent death, but he wasn't about to be positive about anything but the fact that the man was dead."

DeKok smiled. He could well imagine the old man. They had known each other for years and DeKok was extremely fond of the small, always eccentrically dressed, coroner. With his old-fashioned gray spats and striped pants, the decorous morning coat and the greenish Garibaldi hat, the coroner looked like the lone survivor of a previous century. He was extremely competent but his curious behavior and unconventional manners did drive the younger members of the force to distraction.

"Were there any other wounds, I mean, apart from the obvious one on his head?"

"No, other than that he was whole. Not even any scars."

"Tattoos?"

Vledder sighed in exasperation.

"No tattoos, no scars. Just a birthmark on his right shoulder blade."

DeKok rubbed his chin.

"Well," he said, "at first glance it doesn't seem like a whole lot to start a murder investigation with."

Slowly he rose from his chair and started to pace up and down the large detective room. He thought better on his feet. After a while he stopped in front of the window and rocked slowly back and forth on the balls of his feet while he looked at the rooftops of the Quarter where he had spent so much of his life. Whenever his duties allowed, and even when on duty, DeKok liked to walk through the Quarter. He was a well-known figure in the Red Light District of Amsterdam. Everyone knew him and he knew almost everyone. He had the dubious reputation of having more friends in the underworld than in polite society.

It was already getting dark outside and soon the Red Light District would be in full swing and the pace would increase in the police station as well. The old, renowned police station at Warmoes Street, as DeKok liked to think about it. Some referred to it as the Dutch "Hill Street". Among police officers it was known as the busiest police station in Europe, situated on the edge of Amsterdam's Red Light District and hemmed in by the harbor and a polyglot population encompassing all strata of society, from aristocrats to day-laborers and from drug dealers to respectable business people. A hundred or more languages could be heard in the Quarter, churches could be found next to brothels and the bars never closed.

DeKok turned away from the window and raked his fingers through his gray hair. He looked worried but his melancholy face, with the underlying friendliness of a good-natured boxer, always looked somewhat worried. Except when he grinned. When DeKok grinned, few could resist the boyish charm that was then displayed on the craggy face. He stopped in front of Vledder and raised one finger in the air.

"To recapitulate," he said didactically, "we can assume that our friend was hit on the head with some sort of heavy instrument and succumbed thereof. In order to frustrate discovery of the foul deed, a person or persons unknown consequently slipped him into the water of a convenient canal." He remained silent for a while and rubbed the bridge of his nose with a little finger. "That shows a certain amount of coolness under fire. It won't be easy to find the culprit."

Vledder closed his note book.

"Where would you like to start?" he exclaimed emotionally. "We know nothing. We don't even know the name of the victim."

"Come, come," admonished DeKok, "we're policemen, after all. We deal in facts and also detection, deduction and . . . luck."

The phone rang at that moment and Vledder picked up the receiver and listened. Then he gestured toward DeKok.

"It's the desk, downstairs. The sergeant says he has somebody who wants to see you. One Martin Kerkhoven."

DeKok smiled.

"The Slippery Eel. Have him come up."

Vledder passed the message to the desk-sergeant and replaced the receiver.

"Slippery Eel . . . isn't that the nickname of a well-known burglar?"

DeKok nodded.

"In his better days a very competent second-story man, almost an artist in his profession. But lately we haven't heard that much about him."

Vledder looked at his partner with a searching, suspicious look in his eyes.

"Why is he here?"

"I asked him to come."

"Why?"

DeKok scratched the back of his neck.

"To . . . eh, to help us identify the corpse without clues."

"What?"

The old inspector grimaced.

"That's to say . . . I hope so. You see, something immediately caught my eye this afternoon, at the canal. The victim wore Keds, narrow black jeans and a dark turtle-neck sweater. I remembered somebody who would be dressed that way when he swung around the facades and attic windows of our fair city."

Vledder eyes lit up.

"Slippery Eel."

DeKok nodded.

"But, as far as I knew, Slippery always worked alone. A pure individualist in a country full of them. Oh, yes, the very quintessence of individualism, is our Eel. I have never heard that he worked with a partner, not even a look-out. But I found the similarity in clothing a bit too much of a coincidence. That's why I went to Little Lowee."

Vledder grinned.

"The cognac, of course, was merely one of the crosses you had to bear in your tireless search for the truth."

DeKok merely grinned in reply and ignored the remark.

"After some hesitation, Little Lowee told me that Slippery had a partner for a while. A stranger, a mysterious figure who one day, without warning, had descended on the underworld. Anyway," concluded DeKok in a business-like voice, "that's all Lowee knew about him."

Vledder, always ready to jump to conclusions, smiled brightly.

"Our corpse!" he exclaimed.

DeKok raised a cautioning hand.

"Let's not anticipate events. But I thought it *would* be interesting to hear what Slippery has to tell us. There is one additional, significant, detail: the partnership broke up because of a quarrel."

There was a knock at the door. If Vledder had not kept a weather eye on the door, he would not have heard the soft knock over the noise level in the detective room. The shadowy outline of a figure on the frosted glass of the door helped him in identifying a visitor.

"Come in," yelled a detective who was seated closer to the door.

It took a while. Then the door opened slowly and a slender man stood in the door opening. He looked around the room and spotted DeKok. Limping, the visitor made his way across the floor of the large crowded, detective room. DeKok recognized Martin Kerkhoven, better known as Slippery Eel. He looks bad, thought DeKok. It was true. The man's face was gray, his eyes were dull and there was a painful grimace around the mouth.

"Lowee told me that you wanted to see me."

DeKok gave Slippery a friendly nod.

"I want you to meet somebody."

The burglar cocked his head to one side and stared at the gray sleuth.

"Here?"

DeKok shook his head, ambled over to the coat rack, put his little felt hat on his head, hoisted himself into his coat and said:

"Let's go for a ride."

* * *

Vledder drove the police VW to the Pathology Laboratory. He stopped in front of the brick building and waited, his hands loosely on the steering wheel.

Slippery Eel looked at the building and from the building to DeKok, then to Vledder and back again.

"What are we doing here?" he asked with surprise in his voice.

The two inspectors looked back at him but neither answered his question. Instead they got out of the car and with the burglar between them they crossed the wide sidewalk. Vledder punched a code into the electronic lock and they entered. The guard, hidden behind the sports pages in his cubbyhole, looked up and Vledder waved at him in passing.

"Must be the only place where you can work for the police and have a nine-to-five job," grumbled Vledder as they walked through the deserted building.

DeKok did not answer. Neither did the Eel, nauseated by the penetrating smell of disinfectants and formaldehyde that seemed to permeate the building.

Before long they were in the basement. A black-granite table stood almost in the center of a white-tiled room. The naked corpse of the unknown victim had been placed on the table and a sheet covered the corpse.

The two inspectors came nearer the table, Slippery Eel perforce, went with them. He tried to hang back, obviously ill at ease in the forbidding space. But Vledder's hand on one arm and DeKok's hand on the other, forced him, albeit reluctantly, to approach the table. Eel looked paler than before, his nostrils trembled and he tried to swallow a lump in his throat.

DeKok reverently removed his hat and allowed the melancholy expression on his face to dominate. Almost at attention, with bowed head, he stood next to the table. He played the scene with considerable emphasis. It was part of the theatricals that Vledder sometimes so abhorred. DeKok was so obvious, according to Vledder, that it was a marvel that people did not see right through him. But they almost never did.

Sometimes DeKok was really sad, such as now, because the friendly face of the corpse had aroused his sympathy from the beginning. Usually, however, DeKok feigned whatever mood, or state of mind he judged to be the most effective under the circumstance. He could have gone on the stage, thought Vledder.

But the theatricals, whether real or feigned, had a serious purpose. Few murderers could withstand this type of silent confrontation with their victim.

From aside he looked at Slippery Eel. The weak mouth of the burglar trembled. Sweat beaded his forehead. DeKok carefully lifted a corner of the sheet and exposed the face of the victim. Slippery swallowed hard. His tongue darted across dry lips.

"That's . . . eh," he said, "that's Leon."

* * *

They were back in the police station. DeKok pointed to a chair near his desk and Slippery Eel let himself sink into it with a painful grimace. DeKok pulled up another chair and sat down himself. He leaned his elbows on the desk and placed his chin on his folded hands. He grinned at the Eel.

"You saw the hole in his head," he said quietly. "You can hardly try to make me believe you know nothing about it. Everyone knows the two of you had a big fight."

Slippery raised his hands in a gesture of despair.

"That's got nothing to do with it," he exclaimed roughly. "Nothing."

DeKok smiled sardonically.

"And you expect me to believe that?"

The burglar pressed his lips together, narrowed his eyes and stared at his interrogator.

"Suit yourself," he hissed after a while. "I can't make you believe what you don't want to believe. But I can tell you this: I didn't break his head. Perhaps you find this just as hard to believe, but Leon was my friend."

DeKok pushed his lower lip forward.

"A friend who cheated you."

Slippery's eyes spat fire.

"It isn't true!"

DeKok shrugged his shoulders and looked away. Without really noticing it, he observed the usual turmoil in the detective room. It seemed as if he had forgotten all about the burglar next to his desk. Finally he returned his gaze to the Eel.

"Then, why the quarrel?"

The burglar lowered his head.

"He . . . eh, didn't want to follow my . . . eh, my advice. He thought he knew better." Slippery snorted. "Well, you've seen what it got him." There was a sad tone in his voice. "You've seen what it got him," he repeated. He remained silent for a while. Then he continued: "The boy should have listened to me. Then it wouldn't have happened. But they're always so sure of themselves, they always think they know better, before they've had the training, the experience. They think they're invincible."

"What?"

For a moment a wan smile brightened the gray, narrow face of the Eel.

"You know how I make a living?"

DeKok nodded slowly.

"Listen, Eel." His voice was serious and there was no sign of humor in his eyes. "This is different. This is murder. In other words . . . I don't care what you do for a living, as you put it. I'm not interested in catching you for a burglary, or whatever. As far as that is concerned, you don't have to hide anything from me." He gestured toward the burglar. "So, tell me, how was the relationship between you and Leon?"

Slippery Eel sighed.

"You're right. I better tell you the whole story. You see, ever since I fell, I'm no longer too sure of myself. At the most unexpected moments my knees will shake, or I get a cramp. And that's no good in my line of work. That's why I looked around for a partner. Somebody who wanted to learn the profession, so to speak. Well, Leon seemed made for the job. A man with nerves of steel and . . . no reputation, or record. Even you guys didn't know him."

DeKok looked at him sharply.

"How do you know that?"

Slippery grinned.

"During one of our first jobs, he forgot to use gloves. I thought at the time: well, that's it, Leon is off to jail. But the police never came after him." He grinned anew. "You see, that could mean only one thing. You didn't have his fingers on file, or something. My partner was unknown to the police."

DeKok winked at him.

"Excellent, really excellent, I must say. What next?"

The Eel made a melancholy gesture.

"Altogether the partnership lasted just over a month. Then we quarreled. Leon wanted . . ." He did not finish the sentence. His green eyes lit up. Confused, he suddenly looked hard at DeKok. "Has there been a break-in at the Emperor's Canal?" he asked.

DeKok's eyebrows rippled briefly.

"When?"

"Last night."

"Why do you ask?"

"Well, that's what the quarrel was all about. Leon wanted to break in somewhere along the Emperor's Canal. He had a feeling there was quite a bit to haul. But it was a gamble. He had no hard information. Didn't have the gen, as the English say. It could be a bust, in other words. That's why I was against it. I've never, ever gambled like that. First I have to know if it's worth my trouble. Otherwise I'd just as soon stay home. I don't like chances. It's just plain stupid to take risks for nothing. That's what I told him."

"And?"

Slippery Eel spread his arms in a silent appeal for understanding.

"Leon could not be persuaded. He didn't even want to wait. 'If you don't want to come along, I'll go alone. After all, I am not married to you,' he said."

The burglar stared somberly at nothing at all.

"Well," he said after a long pause and a longer sigh, "that was the beginning of the end. We had a real shouting match. I cursed him up one side and down the other. I was furious, you see, because he stubbornly insisted on going his own way. I called him ungrateful. After all, I picked him out of the gutter. Anyway, I called him everything I could think of and told him that it had been a waste of time to try to teach him anything. Finally he walked away mad. I threw a beer glass after him."

"Well?"

"I missed."

DeKok rubbed his face with a flat hand. His brain was trying to assimilate the information. There had to be a clue here. He was missing something. But what?

"Did you know the house where Leon wanted to break in?"

"No, I didn't even want to go look."

"What about the number?"

Slippery Eel, nee Martin Kerkhoven, shook his head.

"He may have told me, but I don't remember. I didn't listen, didn't *want* to listen. I just wasn't interested, you see. I was to decide the jobs, that was our agreement. He was supposed to execute them, but I did the planning. That's why I didn't want to hear about it. I only remember something about the Emperor's Canal."

DeKok nodded his understanding.

"Where did Leon live?"

Again the Eel shook his head.

"I don't know. I've never been at his place. We always met at Little Lowee's."

DeKok stood up. In his typical, somewhat waddling gait he paced up and down the free space in the detective room. Today his walking space was limited to about six paces one way and six paces back. Finally he stopped behind the burglar.

"In any case," he remarked, "our corpse has a name. It's Leon."

"That . . . eh, I don't know."

"What do you mean?"

"I don't know if his name was Leon."

DeKok stepped in front of him and looked at him, apparently confused.

"But isn't that what you said?"

The burglar nodded.

"I called him Leon. Because I thought it fitted him. But what his real name was . . ." Slippery shrugged his shoulders. "I've never heard him say his real name."

3

After Martin Kerkhoven, aka the "Slippery Eel", had left, DeKok ambled back to his desk. His feet hurt. Suddenly he felt tired, bone-tired. As usual, whenever a case was not progressing to his satisfaction, when he found himself on the wrong track, his feet hurt and his legs tortured him. It seemed very early for the manifestation. Usually it happened several days into an investigation, if it happened at all. To be so wrong, so early in the game, was most remarkable. But his feet never betrayed him. Already he must be on the wrong track.

Vledder, who knew the symptoms and the cause, was on the telephone and looked at him with a worried face.

With a painful grimace DeKok lowered himself into his chair and carefully placed his feet on the desk. A hellish pain seemed to tear his calves apart, as if a thousand tiny knives were inserted, twisted and ripped through his muscles. He sat motionless and slowly the pain became less, more bearable, until it almost disappeared.

He leaned back in his chair and looked idly at Vledder behind the next desk. His craggy, melancholy face seemed to get a bit more cheerful as the pain in his legs slowly abated. He reflected on everything that had happened from the initial report of the corpse to the last words of the burglar. He came to the sad conclusion that his legs might have been right with their premonition. It looked like there had been a microscopic amount of progress.

Vledder threw the receiver back on the phone, bringing DeKok back from his musings.

"No burglary?"

Vledder shook his head.

"No they checked all the reports. Plenty of burglaries, but none on the Emperor's Canal, or even near it."

DeKok scratched the back of his neck.

"Too bad," he said pensively. "It might have provided us with some sort of clue, or a starting point." He remained silent for a while, rubbed the bridge of his nose with a little finger. "Although . . . from the fact that no burglary has been reported in that neighborhood, one *could* conclude that our man was bashed on the head *before* the planned break-in."

Vledder moved his chair closer to facilitate communication over the constant background noise of the room.

"But why not?" asked the younger man enthusiastically. "According to the Eel, or at least according to the way he tells it, you would get the impression that one is the result of the other. I mean, that the hit on the head is connected to the plans of his ex-partner. But perhaps there is no connection whatsoever between the contemplated break-in and the murder."

DeKok shrugged his shoulders.

"We just don't know enough," he said, irritation in his voice. "At least, we don't know enough *yet*! That's what got us stumped. It is entirely possible that the Eel is right and that Leon . . . let's call him Leon for the time being . . . that Leon was hit while attempting the break-in. So, we could be looking for a homeowner, or a night watchman in one of the offices. He could have been caught in the act."

Vledder looked at his older colleague with surprise.

"But, surely, in that case the perpetrator would have notified the police? After all, he could always claim self-defense."

DeKok nodded slowly.

"Unless the person was so shocked by his deed that he, or she, panicked and could only think of one thing: *how do I get rid of the corpse?* In that case you can forget about notification to the police. A person like that stays out of sight, keeps his mouth shut. What would you expect? Unless he reports it immediately, it's too late. At least he's likely to think so. Maybe . . . perhaps, in the distant future, he might just make a deathbed confession, or something like that. But that's about it."

Vledder grinned.

"You want to wait for that?"

DeKok could not resist smiling at the ridiculous suggestion.

"I'm afraid that in that case the Commissaris would be the one to panic." He made a questioning gesture. "Did you check on Eel's story about the fingerprints?"

Vledder nodded.

"It checked. The guys from Dactyloscopy compared the fingerprints of our man with 'pending' fingers. They agree with fingerprints found at the scene of a break-in at South Walk Way, about four weeks ago."

"Did they get anything?"

Vledder snorted contemptuously.

"No, it wasn't a big haul. An almost valueless imitation pearl necklace, a few bucks and some coins from a jar used for household money." He grinned. "But a lot of work was accomplished. From the description it seemed more like a training exercise for a beginner, than a real break-in. Of course, that's in retrospect," he added honestly.

DeKok laughed.

"But probably right on the nose. The first lesson for beginners by Professor Slippery Eel. Break-in 101, with lab time." He raked his fingers through his gray hair. "Still," he continued, "it's strange that we *still* haven't identified the corpse. Did you give the description to the press?"

Vledder nodded emphatically.

"Almost immediately after I returned from the lab. It may even have made the evening papers. I would have liked to add a photo of the victim, but the Commissaris wouldn't hear about it. When I proposed it to him, he looked at me as if I had suggested something indecent."

DeKok laughed.

"So, no more than a short notice, for the time being?"

"If, by tonight," said Vledder in the formal, stately tones used by the Commissaris on such occasions, "you have been unable to establish the identity of the victim, I will decide tomorrow if a further dissemination of information via the television networks is desirable."

DeKok grinned. Vledder's imitation of their mutual Chief was uncanny.

"Well, well," he said mockingly, "our boss has made an exceedingly kind qualification."

He looked at the large clock on the wall. It was almost one o'clock in the morning. He waved at Vledder in a gesture of dismissal.

"You better get on home, Dick," he said in a friendly voice. "Get some sleep. But make sure you're on time for the autopsy. It wouldn't do to keep Dr. Rusteloos waiting."

With a remarkably vital motion, considering his recent pain, he lifted his feet off the desk and ambled toward the coat rack. With a nonchalant gesture he place his little hat far back on his head and put on his coat.

Vledder looked at him suspiciously.

"What are you going to do?"

DeKok did not answer at once. Silently he knotted the belt, that almost resembled a twisted rope, around his waist and walked toward the door. There was a pensive look on his face. Then he turned to Vledder who had followed him as far as the door.

"I'm going to have another talk with Little Lowee. He always knows more than you would expect. Maybe *he* can tell me why our dead friend had such an interest in a house at the Emperor's Canal."

* * *

With his hands buried deep into the pockets of his coat and his collar pulled up, DeKok stepped purposely into the direction of Little Lowee's bar. Absent-mindedly he returned the greetings of the pimps on the street corners and the ladies of the evening on display behind their windows. He reflected on the newspaper article he had seen just before he left the station. Someone had left the paper with the desk-sergeant. CORPSE OF UNKNOWN MAN, read the headline. He had noticed it in passing and taken the time to read the article. It was not very long.

Apparently the Commissaris had revealed nothing about the head wound. Not a word about that in the short article. After a mention of the bare facts and a detailed description of the victim, the article had closed with the usual request for information from the public.

DeKok quickened his pace. He had to hurry. During weekdays Lowee almost always closed at one in the morning. If he did not hurry, the bar might be closed. Perhaps he would meet Slippery there as well. In retrospect he had thought up a few more questions . . . questions about Leon, his family, friends, acquaintances, wife, children, girlfriends . . . the man had to have *some* social contacts, after all. Nobody lives in a vacuum. No man is an island, thought DeKok.

Suddenly he heard the clicking of high heels on the pavement behind him. He slowed down and turned around. A woman, dressed in a tight-fitting, red dress had emerged from the "Old Sailors Place" and now approached him. He recognized her at once. Black Sylvia, a former barmaid who was now the sole proprietor of the bar she had just left.

"I just happened to see you pass by," she panted. "So, I thought I'd better ask you."

"What?"

"Well, if it's true that they killed that blond boy."

The gray sleuth pursed his lips. His eyebrows rippled briefly.

"Who says so?"

She gestured with her head.

"Slippery Eel. He said you actually held him for a while, on suspicion."

She hugged herself and shivered in her thin dress.

"Come, DeKok," she said, teeth chattering. "Come on inside. I'll pour you a beer."

Smiling, the inspector followed her.

It was quiet in the "Old Sailor's Place". A lone sailor drowned his sorrow at a table in the back. There was nobody else in the bar. DeKok hoisted himself slowly onto a barstool and watched Sylvia as she tapped the beer. In the sparse lighting of the bar, against the pink and reddish lights she still looked attractive. But he had known her since she first made her appearance in the District and knew she was well in her forties. He liked her. Black Sylvia was not like most of the barkeepers in the neighborhood. She was no hyena who took every customer for the last possible penny. She was more humane, warmer. Maybe too warm, because the number of men in her life could be counted by the score.

"Did you know the blond?"

She placed the beer in front of him.

"It depends what you mean by *know*?" she said laconically. "He stayed in my house for a few days."

"When?"

"About six weeks ago, or so. He came in one night, no coat, wet as a drowned cat and shivering with cold. He asked if he could sit near the stove for a while."

She shook her head.

"Usually I won't allow that. After all, this isn't a hotel. But I noticed at once he was no tramp. I'm pretty good at judging men, if I do say so myself. This guy had class. He hadn't shaved in a week and he looked like hell, but his hands . . . you see, his hands were well kept. You can tell a lot from people's hands."

DeKok sipped from his beer.

"Then what?"

She grinned.

"Well, I gave him a chair next to the stove. Then I fixed him a hot toddy to warm up his insides as well. At first he didn't want it, because he couldn't pay, he said." She cocked her head at DeKok. "So I asked him who was talking about money and he finally accepted it."

DeKok wiped the foam from his mouth.

"So, he was really down on his luck?"

35

She did not react to the remark, but stared dreamily into the distance. DeKok was certain that she had not even heard his question. Her big, brown eyes gleamed with a memory only she knew about.

"He was so damned handsome once he had a chance to shave."

DeKok looked at her searchingly.

""So, you took him home that night?"

With a start she came back to the present..

"What should I have done?" she protested. "Come on, you tell me . . . what should I have done? I could hardly chase him back into the street, now could I? It was raining cats and dogs, it was cold. Where was he supposed to go?"

DeKok nodded. His face was serious.

"You're right," he said solemnly. "Of course. You could hardly chase him back into the night." He gave her a friendly smile. "How long did he stay?"

She shrugged her shoulders.

"About four days," she said carelessly. "Maybe a little longer. I don't remember exactly. But it was nice. I remember *that!* The days flew by." She hesitated. An absent-minded look came in her eyes. "He was totally neglected. He was wearing rags. I bought him some pajamas, underwear, socks, shirts. I still had a suit from an ex-boyfriend. It fitted him to perfection. He left me dressed like a gentleman."

"Why?"

"What do you mean?"

"Why did he leave?"

She smiled a sad smile.

"Who am I? You think I can keep a guy like that?" Her voice trembled with melancholy and regret.

DeKok stretched a consoling hand toward her.

"I would never have left you," he said sincerely.

Flattered, her smile brightened.

"But I must say, he was very nice about it. He told me he couldn't stay any longer, that he had never lived off a woman and that he would be back when it was all over."

They remained silent. DeKok drained his glass.

"What was his name?"

"I called him Jacques."

"Was that his name?"

She shrugged her shoulders.

"I asked him his name. You know, as you do when you meet somebody. He asked me if I thought that important and when I said I didn't care, he asked me to pick a name I liked." She made a simple, graceful gesture. "So I called him Jacques."

DeKok nodded his understanding.

"Did he have a wife, children? Where was he from?"

She shrugged her shoulders.

"I don't know. He never talked about himself. And I . . . I didn't ask."

DeKok shook his head in despair.

"Then . . . what *did* you talk about?" It sounded exasperated.

She laughed with a sexy, chuckling sound.

"You don't have to talk when you do it."

DeKok looked embarrassed.

"I take it," he said with a chilly tone of voice, "that you took time out, for meals and so?"

The cool tone of the inspector drove her sweet memories into the background. Suddenly she was serious.

"I've had this bar for years. Seamen from all over the world come here. Seamen . . . seamen never see a thing. They go everywhere, but never see anything. If you ask a seaman about Hamburg, he'll tell you about the Reperbahn. Ask him about Rio and he'll tell you where to find the brothels. You see what I mean, they never see anything."

"And Jacques?"

A tender smile fled across her face.

"Jacques ... Jacques had been everywhere. Spain, the South of France, Paris ... you name it. Not for a vacation, you know, packed in a touring bus, or with a package group, but for real. You know what I mean? He *lived* there, got to know the people. Jacques had seen a lot ... he could talk about it ... and he did."

"Did you stay home all the time?"

Laughing openly, she shook her head.

"That wasn't possible. After all, I *do* have a business to look after. I open at seven, every night. Jacques would sit at the bar. There, where you're sitting. He chatted with the customers, or played cards. He would help out, tap a new barrel, or something. Sometimes he just went for a walk."

"Did he know people around here, in the Quarter?"

She looked pensive.

"I don't think so. At least, not during the time he stayed with me."

DeKok rubbed the bridge of his nose with a pinky. After a while he looked at the little finger as if he had never seen it before. He studied it, slowly, thoughtfully. He wrestled with a feeling of powerless frustration. The woman across from the bar had been intimate with the man who had occupied his thoughts for hours. And yet the man remained an unknown, a stranger. A stranger without background, without substance, vague. It irritated him greatly. Suddenly he looked up.

"Did you ever notice anything peculiar about him?"

She looked at him, confusion and surprise fighting for supremacy.

"What *do* you mean?"

DeKok made an impatient gesture.

"Did he ever say, or do, anything special. Darn, there's *got* to be *some*thing!"

She did not answer at once. Again she seemed lost in dreamlike memories. The gray sleuth looked at her, hopeful, impatient.

"Wait a minute," she said after a long pause. "You're right. There was something." She chewed her lower lip and placed a hand next to her temple, as if forcing herself to remember. "It was something he said."

"What?"

She closed her eyes.

"It was," she said hesitatingly, "it was the last night he spent at my place. I was already in bed, waiting for him. He was sitting in the big, easy chair next to the window smoking a cigarette. He didn't say a thing. He was more quiet than normal. I'd called him several times, already, but he didn't hear me, as if he was deaf."

"Then what?"

"Then he suddenly said something really odd. He said: 'Can a dead person commit murder?' Yes, that's what he said. 'Can a dead person commit murder?' I'm sure that's what it was."

4

"Can a dead person commit murder?"

Vledder looked up in surprise.

"What did you say?"

DeKok displayed a broad smile. He opened one of the drawers of his desk and took from it a large, blank sheet of paper. With large letters he wrote: Can a dead person commit murder? He looked at it with concentration and spoke every word slowly and emphatically.

Vledder looked confused.

"What brought all that about?"

DeKok grinned.

"It was a question which occupied our friend."

"The man from the canal?"

"Yes, our unknown corpse. Last night I talked to a lady who had extended him her hospitality of room, board . . . and bed."

"Who?"

"Black Sylvia, an old acquaintance of mine. She picked him up about six weeks ago. He was dressed in rags and was broke. She took pity on him and took him home."

Vledder frowned.

"Why? Is she with the Salvation Army?"

DeKok smiled.

"Oh, you cynical person. 'Are there no work houses? Are there no orphanages?', to quote Scrooge." He paused. "No, of course Sylvia isn't with the Salvation Army. But Sylvia *does* have a big heart, overflowing with love for her fellow men. And I do mean *men*. She saw something in him. According to her, our friend had class." He grinned. "And believe me, if Sylvia has an opinion about a man, she knows what she's talking about."

"What did she mean by *class*?"

DeKok made an expansive gesture.

"Position . . . status . . . appearance . . . civilization . . . education . . . rank . . . a man from a good background, from the better circles."

Vledder snorted.

"What's that supposed to mean, *from the better circles*?" His tone was contemptuous. "That's an old-fashioned concept."

Thoughtfully DeKok bit on the cap of his ball-point pen.

"Perhaps," he answered slowly, vaguely. "Maybe . . . Still, in my opinion, it's a good description of the sort of man we're dealing with. I mean, the sort of man he must have been when alive. In any case, despite his association with the Eel, he wasn't just another burglar. If you have to classify him, I would be more inclined to put him in the category of con-men. A wheeler-dealer, the type that goes after millions."

Vledder grinned.

"Stipulating, of course, that he was engaged in crime." DeKok nodded.

"You're right. We can hardly take his abortive stint with the Slippery Eel as proof of a criminal career."

"And Sylvia knew nothing?"

"She called him Jacques, but we may assume that wasn't his real name, either."

"Where did he come from?"

"He told Sylvia that he had spent some time in Spain. Apparently he had also spent some time in France. First in the South and then in Paris. It's possible to conclude that he was fluent in Spanish and French."

"What else?"

DeKok grimaced.

"After a few days of love and bliss he expressed his regrets and told her he couldn't stay any longer. But the parting would not be forever. There would come a time that he would return . . . when it was all over. Black Sylvia didn't take his departing words very seriously. Regretfully she neglected to inquire about the meaning of his words."

Vledder looked at him searchingly.

"That was all?"

"What *do* you mean?"

"Is that all you discovered?" His voice sounded disdainful.

DeKok nodded slowly.

"Indeed," he admitted slowly, "that's all. That's all Sylvia could tell me. I can see that. You mustn't measure women like Sylvia against the normal, more sedate society. Women like Sylvia enjoy such brief affairs. They don't care about the long haul. Actually, the only important statement in her account is the sentence: Can a dead person commit murder?"

Vledder sighed a long-suffering sigh.

"Well, at least that's no problem."

"Oh, why not?"

The young inspector grinned.

"The answer to the question is *No!* Very simple. A dead person is physically unable to commit murder, or anything. In other words ... it can't be done."

DeKok cocked his head at him.

"So, it was a stupid question?"

Vledder did not answer at once. There was an undertone in DeKok's voice that warned him to be careful.

"Yes ... eh," he said, unsure of himself. "I think it was a stupid question."

DeKok pursed his lips.

"Still," he said with a certain emphasis, "still, it's a question that bothered our friend enough that he voiced it. Without volition, do you see? It could be termed the subconscious, spoken conclusion of a specific train of thought. According to Black Sylvia he was so deep in thought that he jumped when she asked him about it. He was rather upset and waved the subject away. When she became curious and wanted to talk about it, he gave clear indications that he didn't want to discuss it. For a moment I contemplated if Sylvia could have misunderstood him. But the strange formulation of the words makes me certain that she must have heard him accurately."

A bit irritated by it all, Vledder shrugged his shoulders.

"I don't know why *you* find it important," he ridiculed. "Me ... I for one, I can't see it. It's a stupid question, stupidly expressed. Of course, you can build up whole castles around it, but that doesn't make it any less stupid. If you're dead you can't commit murder. It's ... it's illogical. It just doesn't compute."

DeKok searched slowly for a stick of gum, found a forgotten piece of hard candy and placed it thoughtfully in his mouth. Then he stared at the ceiling for a while, stuffed the candy into one cheek and looked at his young colleague.

"Sometimes," he remarked mysteriously, "even logic is contradictory to the truth."

Vledder did not react. He was used to DeKok's non-sequiturs. He looked at the large clock on the wall and stood up.

"It's half past nine," he sighed. "I'm going to the autopsy. Anything special you want to know?"

DeKok rubbed his eyes in a tired gesture.

"Ask Dr. Rusteloos if he can estimate the age of the deceased as accurately as possible. These days, what with plastic surgery, it's unwise to depend on just the appearance. Some people look a lot younger than they are. I also would like to know if he consumed any alcohol just before he died and how much."

"That's all?"

The gray sleuth shook his head.

"No, give the good doctor my heartiest greetings and salutations."

Vledder smiled and finished putting on his coat.

DeKok took another look at his piece of note paper.

"Can a dead person commit murder?" he murmured to himself, ignoring the noise level in the busy room. A door slammed, a few computer keyboards and at least one old-fashioned typewriter rattled away and only two desks away three suspects were being interrogated simultaneously. There always seemed to be a ringing telephone somewhere in the room.

"Can a dead person commit murder?" he murmured again. The words seemed to be written in flaming letters. Despite the reluctant attitude of his young colleague, he was convinced that the words had a deeper meaning.

He drummed his fingers on the desk top. What made this particular corpse so mysterious? Why had he hidden his identity, even from Sylvia with whom he had been very intimate, indeed. Was he fleeing something, or someone? Was he hiding from something. Was he wanted by the police? Why? His fingerprints did not appear in the collection of known criminals, at least not in Holland. Unable to answer his own questions, DeKok scratched the back of his neck.

Perhaps something could be achieved via Interpol.* DeKok did not care for Interpol. But they *did* have extensive records. Suppose he circulated the description? Perhaps a photo? And a copy of the fingerprints for good measure? After all . . .

In the midst of his musings he was alerted by a young woman who had entered the large detective room. She was directed from one desk to the next until she stopped in front of DeKok's desk.

DeKok took a good look at her. She was beautiful, he decided, and young. Perhaps twenty, maybe twenty-two years old with big bright eyes and long, chestnut hair that was parted in the middle and framed her face with a particular luster. It gave her a madonna-like appearance. Not a blonde, concluded DeKok, who sometimes had the feeling that in his work he was pursued by beautiful blondes. He did meet a lot of them.

His thoughts had taken less than a fraction of a second. Then he quickly stood up.

---

* Interpol—INTERnational Criminal POLice Organization, to facilitate cooperation and exchange of information between various police forces of most countries in the world. Headquarters are in Paris and the general assembly, the supreme authority in the organization, meets annually in different capital cities. Interpol has its own communication network to various affiliated countries. Interpol specifically does *not* consist of "super" police officers, but acts as a clearing house for information on international crime. Interpol has *no* jurisdiction in its various member countries, but relies on the cooperation of the affiliated police forces.

She smiled shyly.

"Inspector DeKok?" she asked.

"Yes," he answered, "with . . . eh, kay-oh-kay."

With old-world courtesy he came around the desk and seated her on the chair next to it while he adroitly relieved her of a large, rectangular package wrapped in a torn, stained pillow case. He leaned it against the desk and went back to his chair.

She pushed a strand of her long hair from in front of her eyes.

"I've been told that you're in charge of the . . . drowned person, the person who drowned?"

"That's right."

She sighed deeply.

"I saw the article in the paper." She spoke with a definite Anglo-Saxon accent. "And I came at once," she added.

DeKok looked at her searchingly.

"Why," he asked.

She lowered her head.

"I think I can give you certain information."

"Really?"

"Yes, you see, I . . . I went with him." She swallowed. "We dated, I mean, we flirted." She sounded odd. "We . . . loved each other . . . Marcel and I."

"Marcel?"

"Yes."

DeKok looked at her, successfully hiding his surprise. She adjusted her skirt and took the parcel on her lap. DeKok pulled a fresh piece of paper from his desk drawer. He smelled the scent of her perfume and liked it.

"What's your name?" he asked in a friendly tone of voice.

"Mabel . . . Mabel Paddington."

"English?"

A quick smile played around her lips.

"Yes, indeed."

DeKok's face expressed admiration.

"You speak our language very well."

She was visibly flattered.

"My father is British, but my mother is Dutch. She cannot forget her Motherland. I think she tried to teach me Dutch almost from the day I was born. It's because of her that I'm going to school here."

"School?"

"Yes, the University of Fine Arts, the Academy. I . . . eh, I try to paint."

DeKok looked at her from under his eyebrows.

"You try to paint?"

She smiled again, briefly.

"Mother believes I have talent and that I will not get a better education anywhere else but in Amsterdam."

DeKok nodded.

"Where do you live? You rent a room?"

She shook her head.

"No, I live with friends of my parents. The Hoveneer family on the Emperor's Canal. Do you know them? Mr. . . . Charles Hoveneer is supposed to be well known at the Stock Exchange."

DeKok pushed his lower lip forward.

"I'm sorry," he said apologetically, "I don't know him." He made a comical gesture. "Simple cops such as I have little cause to associate with Stock Exchange Tycoons."

She waved nonchalantly.

"It doesn't matter, after all. On the whole, they're very good to me."

DeKok raked his fingers through his hair.

"When did you meet Marcel for the first time?"

"About three, four weeks ago."

"By accident?"

Again she waved nonchalantly in a fleeting gesture.

"Kismet, fate ... what's accident?" She paused and looked thoughtfully over DeKok's head. "I'd been shopping in the 'Beehive'. It was one of my free afternoons, no classes. Before going home I decided to have a cup of coffee in the cafeteria."

"And?"

"Suddenly he was sitting next to me."

"Marcel?"

"Yes. He started to talk to me ... about the weather ... the coffee ... the crowds in the department store. Just casual talk. He had a soft voice with a deep timbre, it was pleasant to listen to him ... so I listened. Maybe I would have ignored him if ... eh, if his eyes hadn't been so blue." She nodded to herself. "It was his eyes, yes, definitely his eyes." She paused again and drifted away into daydreams.

DeKok coughed discreetly.

"He took you home?"

"He carried my parcels. We chatted and made a date for the next day. We have seen each other regularly since then."

"Always in the cafeteria?"

"Yes, in the beginning. Later wherever was convenient. Different places around town."

"When was the last time you saw him?"

"Yesterday. He was really nice. I didn't notice anything peculiar."

"Did he visit you at home?"

49

She looked at the gray inspector. Her large, dark eyes glowed with an inner fire.

"I'm not expected," she said bitterly, "to entertain male visitors in my room."

DeKok pursed his lips.

"I asked you," he said resignedly, "if you received him at home."

She lowered her head. The long, chestnut hair veiled her face like a natural curtain. She did not answer.

"So, he did visit you at home," concluded DeKok.

She nodded slowly, tears in her eyes.

"When there was nobody else at home . . . when they were away . . . I used to invite him in. He posed for me." She raised her head until she looked him full in the face. Her eyes were moist. "My mother," she said softly, "my mother would have allowed it."

"Did you have plans?"

"What do you mean?"

DeKok made a vague gesture.

"It's usual," he said in a friendly voice, "for young people in love to make plans for the future. It's the most natural thing in the world."

A smile broke through her tears.

"We wanted to get married."

"When?"

"When . . . when it was all over."

"What had to happen?"

She did not answer at once. She pulled a handkerchief from beneath the waistband of her skirt and dried her tears. DeKok was charmed by the old-fashioned, graceful gesture. Modern women carried big purses, or kept things in their pockets. Keeping a handkerchief in a waistband reminded him of mothers and grandmothers, of lavender and lace.

"Marcel," she sighed, "was at a decisive point in his life. He called it a time of testing. Once he had overcome that, nothing would stand in the way of our happiness."

DeKok looked at her with a certain amount of suspicion. It seemed to him as if she was reciting a well rehearsed lesson.

"A time of testing?"

She nodded.

"He lived under enormous tension." Again tears filled her eyes. "Poor Marcel, poor, dear Marcel."

She fidgeted nervously with the large parcel on her lap. Awkwardly, with shaking fingers she pushed the pillow case aside. A painting emerged, a forceful painting, executed in vibrant ochers.

With her handkerchief she wiped away a few of her tears that had fallen on the canvas. Then, resting the painting on her knees, she held it up for DeKok to see. Her eloquent hands shook.

"This," she sobbed, "is him."

DeKok looked at the painting in astonishment. He caught his breath. The similarity was uncanny, the expression on the face so real, that it was as if the dead man stared at him in the flesh.

He nodded with open mouth.

"Indeed," he whispered, "that's him."

She lifted the painting from her knees and leaned it carefully against the side of the desk.

DeKok picked it up and placed it flat in front of him on the desk top. Slowly his gaze went over the lines of the face. The bright blue eyes, somewhat dreamy, with a hint of wistful melancholy. The small mouth, playful, almost mocking. The sharp nose, the wide, forceful chin. A remarkable face, friendly, winning, full of longing, full of life.

Suddenly he understood part of the young woman's sorrow. To paint such a portrait, she must have painted with total abandon, as if in a trance. The dynamic of colors, the power of every brush stroke witnessed the loving attention the young woman had lavished on the subject. She had been enthralled and the result almost jumped from the canvas.

"Well done," he sighed. "Extremely well done."

She looked at him.

"I want to see him," she said firmly.

DeKok shook his head emphatically.

"It's not necessary for you to see him. We can forego an official identification. This painting convinces me that we are both speaking about the same man."

Her face became hard.

"I want to see him one more time."

DeKok sighed.

"I really think it better," he said softly and convincingly, "that your memory of him not be ... spoiled by the sight of the body." Almost shyly he scratched the back of his neck, looking for the right words. "He ... eh, he doesn't look that well, you see. There's a wound on his head, a bad one, I'm afraid. His appearance is ..."

"A wound?" she interrupted.

"Yes, a big gash."

She stared at him with wide, frightened eyes.

"Has ... was he ... killed?"

DeKok swallowed.

"Yes, I'm afraid so. We've reason to believe that your Marcel may have been ... murdered. I'm sorry."

Abruptly she jumped to her feet. Her nostrils trembled, her hands shook.

"He's been murdered!?" she screamed. "Somebody killed him!! He's been ..."

Words failed her. DeKok rose hastily and put his arms around her shivering body.

"He . . ." she sobbed. "He's done it after all, the . . . the bastard!"

DeKok brought his mouth close to her ear.

"Who?" he whispered.

"Robert . . . Robert Hoveneer. He *said* he would do it."

5

"He killed him!" Her voice shook and bounced off the bare walls of the detective room. "He ... he ..."

She sobbed soundlessly.

Inspector DeKok pushed her gently back on the chair. Years of experience had taught him to take emotional outbursts with a large dose of salt.

He seated himself opposite her and looked at her tear-stained face. She *seemed* sincere. She really seemed to believe that Robert Hoveneer, whoever *he* was, had killed her friend.

"Why?"

She did not answer. It was as if she had lost touch with reality, as if the world had disappeared, unreachable by the senses. Her mouth fell open and she stared into the distance. Her expression was devoid of all intelligence.

* * *

DeKok waited patiently for her to regain her composure. He pushed his chair a little closer.

"Why?" he asked again. His voice was barely above a whisper, compelling, insistent. "Murder ... murder must have a motive."

She looked at him.

"A motive," she repeated tonelessly. "Of course, a motive. Robert had a motive."

"What?"

She tapped herself on the chest.

"I ... I was the motive."

DeKok nodded with a deep sigh.

"Jealousy!"

She gave him a bitter smile.

"Yes, you could call it that ... jealousy. Almost from the moment I arrived from England, Robert has been pursuing me with his so-called love." She pronounced the last word as if it was something obscene. She paused and stared at the floor. "I have always firmly rejected his advances," she added resolutely.

"Why?"

She shook her shoulders in an irritated gesture.

"I can't help it. I don't like him. He's too, too pushy, too sticky, if you know what I mean. Persistent. But he's not the type of man to look up to ... a man who commands respect." Her lips formed a grin that did not reach her eyes. "Perhaps I'm too old-fashioned. I like strong men, the type of man who can give me the feeling of being protected, sheltered."

"Marcel gave you that feeling?"

She nodded. Her face was serious.

"Very much so. I felt safe with Marcel. He was always so calm, so sure of himself, in command of the situation."

"What's Robert's position in relation to the rest of the family?"

"Robert is the nephew of Mr. Charles. He was a bachelor for a long time, you see. He married rather suddenly, about a year ago. I remember that my mother was a bit surprised, when she heard about it at the time. He was already forty-five." There was something in her tone that implied that forty-five was ancient, past it. DeKok, who was pushing sixty, closed his eyes momentarily. "Alice, his wife, is at least twenty years younger than he is," she added in a tone of indictment.

DeKok said nothing, waited for her to continue. After a while she did.

"Nephew Robert has always been the apple of Mr. Charles' eye. Nothing is too good for him. He pays for his studies, everything. He's been with Mr. Charles since he was sixteen. Mr. Charles looks upon him as if he were his own son."

"How old is Robert?"

"Twenty-eight."

"Not married?"

She smiled faintly.

"No. He says that he's been waiting all his life just for me."

"How did he know about Marcel?"

Her face fell.

"He caught us."

"How?"

She blushed. It made her look lovelier.

"It was rather dumb. I had forgotten to lock the door of my room. Robert came home unexpectedly and, much to his amazement, found my door unlocked."

DeKok's eyebrows rippled, seemed to dance off his forehead. Mesmerized she looked at him. DeKok seemed unaware of the acrobatics performed by his eyebrows as well as the amazement of the girl.

"You said: much to his amazement?" The tone was bland, the eyebrows subsided.

Shaking her head, blinking her eyes as if to clear her sight, she grinned softly.

"I always took great care to keep Robert's amorous inclinations outside my door. I told you he was very persistent."

DeKok smiled.

"How did Marcel react?"

"Oh, very calm. He approached Robert matter-of-factly and asked if it was his habit to enter rooms without knocking."

"What about Robert?"

This time she grinned broadly, a bit maliciously.

"Robert . . . Robert was flabbergasted. His pale, puffy face was as red as a lobster. He looked from Marcel to me. It was obvious he was completely taken aback. By now I knew his various facial expressions. It didn't take long for the astonishment to change to hate. I could see it in his eyes. It seemed an eternity, than he murmured some sort of excuse and disappeared."

Nervously she adjusted the hem of her skirt. DeKok could not help but wonder about the apparent contradictory duality in her. Her hands, her body language, the recent tears, they all spoke of a highly emotional, sensitive woman. But her words were cool and with the exception of a single outburst, very calm and rational. She could have been a policewoman making a report.

"I don't know how it happened," she continued, "I tried to control myself but suddenly I burst out laughing. I just couldn't help myself. Somehow the situation appeared so comical to me, so . . . so ridiculous. I kept laughing, I couldn't stop. Much later I realized that Robert must certainly have taken my laughter as an added insult, as if I were laughing at him."

DeKok rubbed his face as if trying to keep himself awake.

"It *was* humiliating," he said seriously.

She nodded.

"But he took revenge that same evening. At dinner he created a scene in the presence of Mr. Charles and Alice. He mentioned that he was not about to get involved in my 'amorous dalliances', but he gave me the *friendly* advice to be more careful in the choice of my partners. After all, he said in his most unctuous tones, there were quite a number of valuables in his uncle's house and if I made a habit out of inviting every tramp I met . . ."

She lost her poise. She clapped her hands to her face.

"It was terrible. He went on and on. I finally left the table, crying."

DeKok reflected ruefully on his earlier comparison between her and a policewoman. He controlled his impatience.

"I still haven't heard anything about a threat." He could not prevent a slight edge to his voice.

She pressed her lips together, took a deep breath and seemed to regain her composure.

"That came the next day. When I left the house the next afternoon to attend classes, he was waiting for me outside. He asked me if I planned to continue my 'affair' with the man. His words, not mine. His tone was so icy, so insulting, that I would have loved to hit him."

"But you didn't?"

"No, I told him to mind his own business. That my private life was no concern of his."

DeKok nodded encouragement.

"Excellent," he said, "really excellent. Then what?"

"Robert became angry. He grabbed me by the arm and said that he would knock some sense into that tramp if he ever saw me in his company again."

"And?"

She grinned crookedly.

"I ignored him. Marcel and I kept meeting each other."

"Also at home?"

She nodded slowly.

"Yes. Also at home. Usually in the afternoon when I knew that Mr. Charles and Alice would be in town. I wanted to keep them out of it."

"And Robert?"

She rubbed her brow with the back of a hand.

"He warned me one more time."

"When?"

She looked at him, a sad look in her eyes.

"Two days before you found Marcel in the canal."

* * *

"Let's arrest him."

"Who?"

Vledder shook his head at so much obtuseness.

"Who else? Robert Hoveneer, of course!"

With his usual exuberant enthusiasm, Vledder was ready for action. It was odd, reflected DeKok, that he, himself, was widely known as one who disregarded red tape, rules and regulations. But in these sort of situations he usually had to curb the tendency for precipitous action on the part of his young colleague.

"Go on," sighed DeKok.

"Well, there's enough in Mabel Paddington's story to treat him as a potential suspect. Just think. He threatened

to hit Marcel over the head. Well, according to Dr,
Rusteloos, death was virtually instantaneous because of a
blow to the head. Also, Robert Hoveneer has a very strong
motive: hate, jealousy, a lover scorned."

The young inspector raised a warning finger into the
air. Some of the other detectives in the room glanced at him,
but returned to their own work.

"And then there's something else," continued Vledder
with unabated enthusiasm. "The distance from the Hoveneer residence at the Emperor's Canal to the spot where we
found the corpse in the Brewers Canal is less than a hundred
yards as the crow flies. I went to look. The situation is almost
ideal." He paused. "I don't think we're going to find a more
likely suspect in a hurry. One that fits so well in the overall
scheme of things."

DeKok leaned back in his chair.

"Hate, love, passion, murder . . . they're difficult to fit
into the overall *scheme* of things."

Vledder paced agitatedly in front of DeKok's desk.

"But you *have* to do something about it. You can hardly
ignore the girl's story. She clearly points the way to the
murderer."

DeKok did not react. With sublime indifference he
stared at the ceiling. Then he thoughtfully rubbed his chin
and looked at Vledder.

"You went to the autopsy?"

"Yes."

"What did Dr, Rusteloos say about the wound?"

"Deadly."

DeKok nodded.

"You said that. But could he say anything about the
weapon?"

Vledder plopped down behind his own desk and shrugged his shoulders. He was clearly irritated. He had a petulant look on his face. Obviously he was not at all pleased with DeKok's changing of the subject.

"A metal bar," he growled reluctantly, "or something like that. According to Dr. Rusteloos the blow was administered from behind. The murderer must have stood *behind* his victim."

DeKok looked at him in astonishment.

"*Behind* the victim?"

Vledder nodded.

"Yes, from behind and above. Most likely at a time when the victim was below the killer. Seated, for instance. Dr. Rusteloos mentioned the possibility that both could have been walking down stairs. The victim up front, obviously."

DeKok rubbed the corners of his eyes.

"Heart trouble?"

"No."

"Alcohol?"

"Minimal. Less than two five per mille."

DeKok sighed.

"Point oh two five. Not much, but it means that he must have had one or two stiff drinks before he died."

Vledder nodded silently.

"Anything else?" prodded DeKok.

Vledder shook his head.

"Dr. Rusteloos estimated the age of the victim around thirty years old. Estimating the age was as difficult for him as for us." He shrugged his shoulders nonchalantly. "The autopsy did not reveal anything startling. In a matter of speaking it just confirmed the opinion of the coroner, the man was dead before he hit the water."

DeKok stared at nothing in particular.

"But it's now certain that he was murdered." He smiled ruefully. "If we only knew the name of the victim . . . we could perhaps deduce the name of the suspect."

Vledder looked at him in genuine surprise.

"But don't you know yet? The name, I mean?"

"No."

"But . . . what about Mabel Paddington?"

DeKok smiled.

"Mabel was too much in love to look closely."

"What do you mean?"

"Well, she lived from one date to the next. It was enough for her that the love of her life was called Marcel. She never asked further."

Vledder snorted.

"That's incredible. She couldn't tell you anything at all?" There was disbelief in his voice. "I mean what was his family name, where did he work, where did he live, where did he come from?"

DeKok shook his head slowly.

"No, she seemed genuinely shocked when I asked, casually, if Marcel was married. She had never even considered the possibility. I think my question spoiled her memories somewhat."

"Stupid girl," hissed Vledder. "If she had kept her lover outside the house, nothing would have happened."

DeKok looked at him with a resigned look on his face.

"So, you insist there is a clear connection between Mabel's love affair and the murder?"

Vledder took the challenge. He pushed his chin forward and the look in his eyes dared DeKok to disagree.

"Yes, I do." It sounded arrogant. "And if you won't do anything about Robert Hoveneer, I will."

DeKok cocked his head at his colleague. There was a smile on his face.

The phone rang suddenly. DeKok picked up the receiver and listened. Dompeler, the acting Watch Commander was at the other end of the line.

"There's somebody down here asking for you. A young man ..."

" ... with a pale, puffy face," supplied DeKok.

Dompeler laughed.

"You're right, it describes him to a tee."

"Very well, let him come up."

DeKok replaced the receiver with a tender gesture and waved vaguely in the direction of Vledder.

"Prepare yourself."

"What for."

"To do something about Robert Hoveneer."

Vledder looked at him, momentarily confused.

"The murderer?"

DeKok nodded.

"Robert Hoveneer ... is on the way up."

6

The man who entered the detective room a little later was big, wide and ponderous. His face, although undeniably pale and puffy, was friendly and round, crowned by a crew-cut that almost reached his eyebrows in front and seemed to disappear to nothing at all over his ears. With a wide smile on his lips, he maneuvered his way through the desks in the direction of Vledder and DeKok. His fleshy cheeks quivered with every step.

Inspector DeKok came from behind his desk and stretched out his hand. Meanwhile he looked searchingly at his visitor. At first glance the man gave a comical, almost naive impression. But alert eyes glittered from behind the strange, small spectacles with the wire frame.

"Robert Hoveneer?"

The round face expressed surprise.

"Yes."

DeKok gave him a winning smile.

"My name is DeKok, DeKok with . . . eh, kay-oh-kay. This is my colleague Vledder," he gestured toward the young inspector. Then he turned back to look at his visitor. "To what do we owe the pleasure of your visit?" he asked politely.

The young man swallowed.

"How do you know my name?"

DeKok shrugged his shoulders.

"It's inherent in my profession," he said, "to always be informed as much as possible."

Hoveneer nodded slowly.

"I understand," he said even more slowly. "And I think I know the source of your knowledge," he added.

"Really?"

The heavy-set young man sighed.

"I have a suspicion that you may have learned a thing or two about me from Mabel Paddington."

DeKok grinned broadly.

"Yes, indeed. Mabel Paddington. She was extremely forthcoming."

Robert Hoveneer showed a tired smile.

"That's the reason for my visit. I'm afraid she may have told you things that are not exactly truthful . . . Lies, not to put too fine a point on it. Lies that are designed to place me in a less than auspicious position."

DeKok pointed at the chair next to his desk.

"Please sit down."

"Thank you."

DeKok waited patiently until the young man was seated.

"Why would Mabel do such a thing?" he asked in a friendly tone of voice.

Robert Hoveneer shook his head dejectedly.

"It's hard to say," he said hesitantly. "I really don't know exactly. The last few days Mabel hasn't been herself. She almost slinks through the house, jumps at the slightest noise and doesn't talk to anyone. She's obviously under stress. I don't know why, but it explains her behavior."

"That's circular reasoning. She's under stress and that's why she behaves the way she does and that's why she's under stress? Come now, there has to be a better reason."

"Well, it's fear."

DeKok looked at him sharply.

"Fear . . . of what . . . of whom?"

"Fear of me. She's afraid of me. She thinks I have killed that man . . . that . . . that Marcel."

"And that isn't true?"

The question was particularly laconic.

Robert Hoveneer laughed. A nervous, hiccuping laugh without mirth.

"Of course, it isn't true. It's downright ridiculous. Mabel Paddington is crazy. Why would I want to kill the man?"

DeKok did not answer. He looked evenly at the young man. Hoveneer's face showed an expression of beguiling naïveté. But the eyes remained alert.

DeKok wondered how this large, and undoubtedly strong, man would react in anger. Most likely in a sudden explosion of strength. He glanced past his visitor and looked at Vledder. He knew that Vledder was eager to take over the interrogation. Slowly DeKok rose from his chair and gave Vledder unspoken permission to go ahead.

* * *

Vledder pushed his chair closer and sat down with his arms resting on the back of the chair. Supporting his head on his balled fists he looked at Hoveneer for a while.

"But didn't you have a motive?" asked Vledder after a long silence.

Hoveneer looked at him with genuine astonishment.

"Me . . . a motive?"

Vledder grinned maliciously.

"You can hardly deny that Marcel was in your way. As long as he was around your advances toward Mabel would be fruitless." He paused and looked intently at his victim. "After all," he added, "you're in love with Mabel, aren't you?"

Hoveneer bowed his head.

"I love her," he said simply. "I try to fight it, but it isn't possible. I can't fight my feelings."

"Thus . . . a motive."

The young man looked up sharply.

"It wouldn't have taken long. Mabel would have discovered soon enough that he was nothing but a tramp. There was no reason whatsoever for me to kill him. I just had to make sure that her eyes would open, that she would realize what he was."

"Nothing else?"

"No."

Vledder leaned forward.

"Why," he asked vehemently, "did you threaten to bash in his skull?"

Hoveneer's face changed. All naïveté had gone from his expression. His face became a hard mask, without any expression.

"She didn't want to listen to me," he said finally, emotionally. "Whenever I started to discuss Marcel, she would clap her hands over her ears like a child and she would run away. It was enough to drive one to distraction. Believe me, at heart Mabel Paddington is a nice, sweet and intelligent girl, but that guy seemed to be able to make her lose all sense of propriety. It was as if she was bewitched."

Vledder nodded understanding.

"Mental dominance," he said wisely.

The young man pressed his lips together.

"Yes," he hissed, "you could call it that, mental dominance. But negative, completely negative. That guy awakened her lowest instincts."

"Really?"

"Yes, how else would you explain it?"

Vledder shrugged his shoulders.

"Love?"

Robert Hoveneer snorted contemptuously.

"Love . . . it had nothing to do with love! That guy was no more than a parasite, he preyed on her . . . on the budding passions of a young, inexperienced girl. He was a bastard without any morals, without a conscience."

Vledder rubbed his chin in a subconscious imitation of one of DeKok's gestures.

"It put you in a difficult position."

"Me?"

"Yes, after all, the duty, the obligation to protect Mabel from the dangers of Marcel rested with you. It was your moral duty to warn her, wasn't it?"

The young man flicked a quick tongue along his dry lips.

"Yes . . . that's to say . . . yes, I felt it that way."

Vledder nodded as if he had known it all along.

"Exactly. And when, despite your well-intentioned warnings, she persisted in ignoring you, just wouldn't listen to your advice, you had no other choice . . ."

"What do you mean?"

The young inspector looked sharply at him.

"One night you followed him and bashed in his head."

Shocked and infuriated, Hoveneer jumped to his feet. His cheeks were deep red. There was a wild look in his eyes.

"No, dammit, no," he yelled. "I didn't kill that . . . that . . . "

"But you had every reason."

Hoveneer pressed his lips together and balled his fists until the knuckles showed up white. His gray-greenish eyes lit up behind his strange glasses. It lasted several seconds and then he relaxed. Slowly the red drained from his face and the fire in his eyes dimmed. He relaxed his fists and with an effort he regained control of himself. He pulled up his chair and sat down.

"I understand," he sighed, "that in your eyes I had a clear motive . . . hate, jealousy. I also understand that you see me as a potential murderer and that this interrogation is designed to make me confess . . ."

Vledder raised a restraining hand.

"To bring out the truth," he corrected sharply.

"All right, all right," said Hoveneer hastily, "for the sake of truth. But it would be a very convenient truth for you if I had killed Marcel."

Vledder nodded.

"Yes," he answered simply.

Robert Hoveneer sighed again.

"I'm sorry to have to disappoint you. I repeat for the last time: I did NOT kill that man! If this interrogation were to go on for hours, days, weeks even, you would not get any other answer from me."

Vledder pushed his chin forward in a challenging gesture. His nostrils trembled slightly.

"That," he said vehemently, "remains to be seen. Where were you Monday night?"

Robert Hoveneer grinned. It was not a pleasant sight.

"You want an alibi?"

"Exactly."

Slowly he shook his head.

"I'm afraid," he said in a regretful tone of voice, "that I don't have an alibi. Last Monday night I went to the movies. Alone."

"Where?"

"Tuschinsky. Second performance. It started, I think, around nine-fifteen. I saw *Bram Stoker's Dracula*, the new version. I'll tell you the story, if you want. I remember it very well, especially Anthony Hopkins, he played a Dutchman, you know."

Vledder shrugged his shoulders.

"That means nothing. You could have seen the movie at any time. You could have read the book, or seen an earlier version. Even if you had a ticket . . ."

" . . . I could have picked it up anywhere." Hoveneer nodded to himself. "I understand, the possession of a ticket does not prove that one has attended the performance." He smiled suddenly. He seemed genuinely amused. "Therefore, no alibi," he concluded. "Now what?"

"You went straight home after the performance?" asked Vledder.

"Yes."

"About what time was that?"

"Nearly midnight. It's a long movie, you know. I remember looking at the clock of the Wester Church."

"Did you meet anyone in the street?"

"No, nobody. That's to say, nobody I knew. It wasn't all that busy in the streets. I walked home along the canals. I went straight to my room."

"Was anybody still awake when you came home?"

"I don't know. As far as I remember there were no lights on anywhere. But it's possible that Uncle Charles, or Alice, still had guests. They usually go to bed late."

71

"Was Marcel with Mabel?"

Hoveneer's face became rigid. Again the blood rose to his cheeks.

"How should I know?" he exclaimed.

"But didn't you check up on her?" asked Vledder innocently.

Again Hoveneer sprang to his feet. He did it so abruptly that the chair clamored against the floor.

"I . . . I . . . refuse," he stuttered, "I refuse to answer any more questions."

DeKok came closer and righted the chair.

"What my colleague means," he said soothingly, in a calm, gentle tone of voice, "is that your feelings for Mabel Paddington caused you to be especially alert regarding her relation with this Marcel. You were, . . . eh, attuned to her, so to speak. Isn't that so?"

Robert Hoveneer stared at DeKok with a suspicious look in his eyes, he seemed to taste the words, examine them for hidden barbs. But he could only detect genuine concern, real interest. Little did he know that DeKok could be a consummate actor whenever he felt like it. Robert had not the slightest inkling that the gray sleuth did not trust him. DeKok never trusted men who displayed such a range of seemingly contradictory emotions in such a short time.

All that went through Vledder's mind. Vledder knew DeKok very well. He waited expectantly for further developments. Hoveneer took another long look at DeKok.

"Well," he said finally, hesitatingly, a bit sheepish, "well, to tell the truth, my concern for her *was* mixed with a certain amount of egotism."

DeKok nodded emphatically.

"Understandable . . . completely understandable, very human. But yet," he went on in an unctuous tone of voice that only Vledder seemed to hear, "I have to assume that you didn't call Mr. Marcel a tramp, or a, what was the word, a parasite for nothing? You must have had a reason."

Robert Hoveneer hesitated visibly. With slow movements he removed his glasses, took a silk handkerchief from his breast pocket and started to clean them with it. After a long silence he spoke again.

"Marcel," he said somberly, "*was* a tramp. Even if he had not been involved with Mabel, if Mabel had not been infatuated with him, I would have warned her about him. You understand? I would have considered it my duty."

DeKok looked at him with surprise on his face.

"You knew him?"

The young man replaced his glasses and shook his head.

"I didn't know him. I never spoke with him."

Vledder watched intently as DeKok's eyebrows suddenly seemed to dance right off his forehead. Even Hoveneer seemed momentarily taken aback. He looked at the old inspector as if he was someone from another planet. The fleeting impression was gone before Hoveneer could convince himself that he had seen what he had seen. Vledder smiled to himself.

"But you called him a tramp," insisted DeKok.

Hoveneer sighed.

"One Wednesday afternoon," he began in a mock patient tone of voice, "I think about three weeks ago, I heard voices when I came home. The voices came from Mabel's room. I thought it rather strange. Mabel never had visitors. As far as I knew she had no friends or relatives in the city. At least I had never heard anything about that. Anyway, I carefully opened her door and I saw Mabel. She was in the company of a man. Later I heard his name was Marcel."

He paused, made a gesture as if he was going to clean his glasses again, but caught a stern look from DeKok. Instead he continued.

"The situation," he said, "was rather compromising. I was too stunned to say anything at the time. You understand? I was shocked, had not expected anything like that. I felt miserable. In a panic I fled to my own room and contemplated what to do. I had always seen Mabel's attitude toward me as a game, a tease. I had never, in my wildest imagination, considered another man in her life . . ."

He broke off, swallowed and then seemed to find the strength to continue. It was a masterful performance, thought Vledder.

"After a while," continued Hoveneer," I carefully left my room and sneaked out of the house. I took a position along the edge of the canal, between some cars and decided to wait for the man to leave."

"And?"

"It took almost two hours. Then they both appeared at the door and kissed each other goodbye. Then Mabel went back inside and the man disappeared in the direction of the Brewers Canal. I watched him carefully, studied him . . . his gait, his clothing. When he was about to turn the corner, I followed him. I wanted to know what sort of man he was."

"Go on," urged DeKok.

"Well, he walked across the Gentlemen's Market, via the Dam to the New Dike and from there into the Quarter, the red-light district. I became more curious with every step. I could hardly wait to find out where he was going. Every once in a while he would wave cheerfully to some whore and once to a provocatively dressed woman in a bar. Then he turned onto the Rear Fort Canal. I stayed at one side of the canal when he crossed the bridge. Much to my amazement he entered a flop house."

"A flop house?"

"Yes, *The Blue Pitcher.*"

DeKok had seated himself on the edge of his desk. Hoveneer was still standing. DeKok looked up at him with a sweet smile on his face.

"And then," said DeKok with just a hint of sarcasm, "you decided that the man had to be a tramp."

Hoveneer felt the correction.

"I didn't come to that conclusion all at once," he answered moodily. "Since that Wednesday afternoon I've been to the Rear Fort Canal several times. I saw him almost every time, and at different times of the day. He certainly didn't do any regular work and really seemed to live in that filthy flop house." He looked at DeKok with an unpleasant grin on his face. "Perhaps you would have come to another conclusion?" he challenged.

DeKok made a vague gesture.

"To you, Mr. Hoveneer, he was a tramp, a parasite, a drifter."

"Exactly."

DeKok nodded thoughtfully.

"A man," he said resignedly, "who could be killed without too much fuss, who could be bashed over the head without burdening your conscience."

7

Vledder laughed.

"My, my, my, what a noise that guy made! When you, too, accused him of murder, I thought he was going to have a heart attack."

DeKok affected a look of utter innocence on his face.

"I had to try," he excused himself.

Vledder narrowed his eyes thoughtfully.

"You went about it in rather a sneaky way," he admired. "Your last remark sort of broke the camel's back."

DeKok rubbed the back of his neck.

"The man irritated me, that was all. The denigrating way he spoke about the deceased felt wrong somehow. He did not have the right to make such a judgement. It bespoke a narrow-minded, middle-class, bourgeois morality. Just because the man stays in what he terms a flop house, doesn't make him a tramp. Everybody sometimes gets a bad break, some of us go broke."

Vledder's face was serious when he answered.

"You're right. Besides, he tried to make out like he was the protector of Mabel's virtues while in reality, he had the same objectives. His story is full of hate and jealousy. No matter how he tries to disguise it."

"Also," said DeKok, as if it made a lot of difference, "I didn't care for his mood swings."

"I knew that," answered Vledder.

DeKok pulled thoughtfully on his lower lip while staring at nothing in particular.

"Still," he said after a long pause, "I'm not at all convinced that Robert Hoveneer is the killer. To be honest, I don't think he's the sort of man to go to such extremes. You see, despite the hate and the jealousy, Marcel was no real threat to him. At most he was a rival in love, a competitor, for the charms of Mabel. Also, I couldn't catch him in a single lie, on the contrary, his story *is* believable. Especially his story about shadowing Marcel sounds true to form. We can safely assume that our corpse lived in *The Blue Pitcher* for a while."

Vledder shook his head.

"I still find it hard to understand that neither the Eel, nor Sylvia, could tell us that their Leon, or Jacques, stayed at *The Blue Pitcher*. Mabel Paddington seemed to be unaware of it as well. At least, she didn't mention it."

DeKok shrugged his shoulders.

"It's possible that our dead friend was embarrassed and didn't want anyone to know he was staying in a cheap hotel, really no more than a boarding house, at the Rear Fort Canal. Let's face it, it's not exactly an up-scale neighborhood and although *The Blue Pitcher* is not exactly a flop house, it's also not what you would call a prestigious address."

Vledder cocked his head at his older colleague.

"And that," he said with a mocking tone in his voice, "is evidence of a narrow-minded, bourgeois mentality."

DeKok laughed out loud.

"Come on," he said cheerfully, "put your coat on. We're going to see Uncle Steven Blader."

Vledder looked at him in surprise.

"Who's Uncle Steven Blader?"

"The owner of *The Blue Pitcher*. I would just love to know under what name Marcel was registered."

* * *

"Uncle" Steven Blader used a greasy cloth to wipe a few spots off a rough, wooden counter, pushed some nickels and dimes into a drawer with fingers that were distorted from rheumatism and picked up a cigarette that was scorching the edge of the counter. Only then did he look up. Recognition dawned in the tired eyes, caught in a web of fine wrinkles.

"Good morning, Mr. DeKok," he said hoarsely. "Haven't seen you for a long time." He brought the butt toward his mouth and dragged his lungs full of smoke.

"You come for the register?"

Without waiting for an answer, he picked up a grubby book from behind a coffee pot and threw it nonchalantly on top of the counter.

"They're all in there. Right up-to-date. Even those for tonight have been entered."

DeKok opened the register and let his fingers do the walking along the names of guests.

"You're right, it's right up-to-date. Excellent," he said approvingly, "really excellent." Then, casually, he asked: "Any deaths, lately?"

Uncle Steven looked at the ceiling as if the answers were written there.

"Let's see," he answered, without lowering his gaze, "Old Walter Knut was the last one. You remember, the one who drank de-natured alcohol, fuel really."

DeKok nodded with a somber face.

"I heard he was dead."

The hotel keeper grinned sadly.

"Yes, we found him in the morning, on the floor next to the bed with a wrinkled obituary card in his hands." He lowered his gaze to look at the DeKok.

"Obituary card?" asked DeKok.

"Yes, the one they printed for his old mother. He always kept it. He showed it to everybody, whether they wanted to see it, or not. Everybody had to read it."

"The obituary notice?"

"Yes, if they didn't want to read it, he'd read it to them. Sometimes he would sit for hours with the notice in his hand, just staring at it. He must have known he wasn't going to be much longer for this world. You understand, he wanted to keep it handy, just in case."

DeKok bit his lower lip.

"Walter Knut . . . God rest his soul."

Uncle Steven nodded devoutly in agreement. Then his mood changed.

"How about some coffee?" he asked. "Just fresh."

"All right, pour away. But I really came about the blond guy who checked in about three weeks ago."

The old man manipulated coffee pot and mugs with much practiced ease, despite his rheumatic hands.

"You mean Marcel Duval?"

"Was that his name?"

Uncle Steven shrugged his shoulders while managing to keep the stream from the coffee pot perfectly steady.

"That's what it says in the register. Born in France, in St. Etienne. The mother is Dutch and the father is French."

"How do you know?"

"He told me. He told me he had just arrived from France and was looking for his cousin in Amsterdam."

DeKok looked incredulous.

"He was looking for who?" he asked.

"His cousin. The daughter of his mother's eldest sister. Apparently the child must have married some rich geezer in Amsterdam."

"What did he want from his cousin?"

"Some hospitality, I think."

DeKok grinned.

"A nice story."

Uncle Steven slurped from his coffee. Then he replaced the mug on the counter.

"You know how it is, Mr. DeKok," he said. "I'm not exactly in the Michelin Guide. I have a hotel, some call it a flop house. All right, most of my guests sleep three or four to a room. But it's reasonably clean, cheap and I don't allow no monkey business. But all of my guests have their stories. Why should I doubt them, why should you care. Sometimes it's the only thing they have left. I'm the last refuge of the hopeless. From here they go on welfare . . . or worse. But some make it back. Sometimes all they need is a helping hand. More power to them, I say."

DeKok looked serious. The old man had not left him unaffected.

"Did he mention the name of this cousin?"

The old man shook his head.

"He didn't know her name. That's what made it so difficult. All he had to go on was his mother's name. He never did know the married name of his aunt. He also didn't know the name of the man his cousin had married."

DeKok grimaced.

"It's all a bit vague, don't you think?"

Uncle Steven pushed his lower lip forward which gave his stubbly face a peculiar look, since he wasn't wearing his teeth.

"At Town Hall they told him they couldn't help him. I advised him to place an ad in some of the larger dailies."

"And?"

Old man Blader shrugged his shoulders.

"I don't know if he did that. I haven't seen him since." Suddenly he looked sharply at Vledder and DeKok. "Why all this sudden interest," he asked suspiciously. "Is something wrong with the boy?"

"He's dead."

"Dead?"

DeKok nodded slowly.

"Murdered. We fished him from the Brewers Canal, last Tuesday. They banged him on the head with a piece of pipe."

The hotel keeper looked confused.

"Really?" There was disbelief in his voice.

DeKok took a careful sip of the hot coffee.

"It's no use to tell you stories," he said laconically. "That's not what they pay me for. The boy is dead. Didn't you read it in the papers?"

Uncle Steven shook his head.

"I don't read newspapers. Too busy. I simply lack the time."

He looked somberly into the distance.

"Nobody told me anything," he said musingly. "Usually I hear those things. You hear a lot of gossip in my job." He pressed his lips together, almost making his toothless mouth disappear. "Marcel," he sighed. "Poor boy . . . murdered . . . by whom . . . and why?"

DeKok grinned.

"You tell me. I would be most obliged."

The hotel keeper nodded his understanding. Lost in thought, he stared at his coffee mug. Suddenly he looked up.

"When did you say he was killed?"

DeKok scratched the back of his neck.

"Well, I can't tell you the exact time of death. But we found him around ten in the morning on Tuesday. According to the coroner he had been in the water for more than twelve hours. Therefore we *guess* that he was killed Monday night, or early Tuesday morning."

Uncle Steven screwed up his face into impossible wrinkles.

"That's weird," he said at last.

"How's that?"

"Well, Tuesday night there was a guy here to pick up Marcel's belongings."

DeKok swallowed.

"His belongings?" he asked.

Uncle Steven nodded.

"Yes, Tuesday night. It must have been around eight o'clock. It was a gentleman, at least, by sight. He said that he came to pay Marcel's bill and would take his belongings at the same time."

"Why?"

The old man shrugged his shoulders.

"He said that Marcel had sent him. Apparently he had found a different place to stay."

"Where?"

"I don't know. The guy didn't tell me. I didn't ask."

"Why not?"

"He was a phony. I knew that right away. Marcel had never sent him."

DeKok looked at him, confusion on his face.

"How ... how did you know he was a phony?"

"Marcel didn't owe anything. Marcel never owed anything. He always paid in advance."

DeKok grinned.

"So you didn't hand over his ... eh, his belongings?"

"Of course not. Anyway ... Marcel had no belongings, no luggage. At least, I never saw any. His closet is empty."

"Did you say that to the man?"

"No, I just did as if I didn't notice a thing, I just acted stupid, as if I hadn't figured him out. I quietly got rid of him. I told him that Marcel had to come himself to get his stuff."

"Then what?"

"He went away."

"Just like that?"

"What do you mean?"

DeKok sighed.

"Didn't you ask him his name?"

"Yes, of course." The hotel keeper gummed his cheeks pensively. "It was a strange name. Wait a minute, he gave me a card."

The old man pulled open a drawer below the counter. His rheumatic fingers searched among some papers.

"Here it is," he said with a note of triumph in his voice.

DeKok took the card from him.

Charles Hoveneer, he read, *Licensed Stock Broker*.

8

The high, bluestone steps of *The Blue Pitcher* were shiny from the rain. The water descended steadily from the heavens. The weather had changed completely since Vledder and DeKok had first fished the corpse from the canal. The mild spring sun had disappeared, locked away behind dark thunder clouds. It seemed as if Mother Nature had skipped summer altogether and had moved directly from spring to the miserable, cold, wet autumn that so often characterizes the weather in Holland.

DeKok pulled up the collar of his coat and pushed his old, decrepit felt hat deeper over his eyes. His face showed deep creases and there was a thoughtful look in his eyes. He had been touched by the conversation with the boarding house owner. And it made him wonder.

He could understand how Robert Hoveneer, driven by jealousy and hate, had been interested in the deceased. But what about Uncle Charles? He just did not seem to fit into the overall picture. It did not compute, as Vledder was wont to say. Why would Charles Hoveneer be interested in the belongings of a dead man?

And who *was* the corpse? Was his real name Marcel Duval? Or was that another alias? Did he indeed come from

St. Etienne in France? Who was the cousin? Why would he have come to Amsterdam to seek her out, if he was not even sure of her name? Did she exist? Or was it another figment of his imagination? Like his many names? DeKok sighed. The mysteries around the corpse seemed to multiply with every step.

Deep in thoughts of his own, Vledder walked beside him. His restless, inquiring mind played several possibilities and scenarios against each other. He, too, seemed to be occupied with a wide assortment of possibilities and questions. Suddenly the younger man stopped.

"He's going to be buried tomorrow, right?"

DeKok rubbed the rain from his face and looked back at him.

"Yes," he answered, "at ten o'clock at Saint Barbara's."

Vledder nodded.

"Suppose . . . we call a few reporters. You know, some of those we know. Brakel, Lammers, Vugt . . . then we have all the large dailies and we ask them if they want to do something special about the case. After all, murder isn't your everyday crime in Holland. It happens more often than in the past, but still, it's major news. Perhaps we can get some headlines: Funeral of Mysterious Corpse, or something."

"But why?"

"It's more effective than an advertisement. Perhaps the cousin he was looking for, will step forward. I wouldn't mind meeting her. Perhaps his death is connected to the fact that he was looking for her."

DeKok looked intently at his assistant.

"I don't follow you."

Vledder gesticulated.

"Perhaps the cousin doesn't want to be found at all," he said impatiently. "Maybe, for whatever reason, she isn't too happy about people looking for her."

Thoughtfully DeKok pulled his lower lip. He let it plop back. The usually annoying sound was drowned by the sound of the falling rain. Nevertheless he repeated the gesture several times.

"And what about the Hoveneer family?" he asked after a long pause while both men were being soaked by the rain.

"Forget them, they're not involved."

Despite the moment and the weather, Vledder was momentarily fascinated as DeKok's eyebrows suddenly seemed to play tag with the raindrops. The phenomenon disappeared as quickly as it had started.

"Well, well, well," mocked DeKok, "and I thought you had already tagged Robert Hoveneer as the suspect."

Vledder shook his head emphatically.

"Believe me," said Vledder urgently, "neither Robert, nor his uncle Charles have anything to do with it. Their interest in Marcel is only marginal, mainly because of the amorous relationship with Mabel."

DeKok nodded slowly.

"It's a fine theory. But if the unknown cousin, according to you, is willing to commit murder in order to remain undiscovered, I somehow doubt that she'll come forward voluntarily."

Vledder grinned. It made his face look demonic in the dripping rain.

"Marcel is dead. Perhaps she won't mind being found."

DeKok pushed his hat further back on his head. The rain beat against his face and the brim of his hat acted as a gutter, pouring water down his back. Both men seemed oblivious to the weather. Only Dutchmen and people from the Pacific Northwest could so completely ignore a downpour.

"All right," said DeKok resignedly. "Go ahead. See what you can do with the press." He rubbed his chin. "And when you're on the phone anyway, call the police in St. Etienne. Ask if they know a Marcel Duval. Be sure to give *all* particulars. The Dutch mother, the date of birth from the register ..." He stopped without completing the sentence and smiled at Vledder. "Anyway," he concluded, "you know what I mean. Polish your best French. Good practice for you. Avoid Interpol, please. They take too long and I would rather go to the source, now that we possibly have one."

It was Vledder's turn to smile. He knew that DeKok did not care for Interpol. He often suspected that it was because of the plethora of modern communication methods used by that International Police Organization. DeKok abhorred all modern communication devices. Considered them an invasion of privacy. If somebody really wanted to get in touch with you, so argued DeKok, they should take the trouble to write a letter, or visit you in person. All this went through Vledder's mind, while he threw a mock salute.

"*Oui, oui, mon patron,*" he said with an atrocious French accent.

DeKok ignored the by-play with supreme indifference. He slowly turned around and walked on. Vledder followed. They left the Rear Fort Canal and crossed forgotten parts of the red-light district. After a while they turned a corner and found themselves in front of the *Old Sailor's Place*. DeKok stopped in front of the locked door and rapped the glass with his knuckles.

Black Sylvia, dressed in a light-blue smock, a dishrag over one shoulder, opened the door with a smile.

"You're coming to tell me you found him?"

"Found who?"

"Who else? The killer of Jacques."

DeKok shook his head.

"We do our best," he answered. "But things don't move as fast as you think, or I would wish." He pointed at Vledder. "Have you met my colleague? He's the most handsome one in our inventory. We generally only use him for cases involving single women."

Sylvia laughed. It made her look twice as young and three times as attractive. She stretched out a friendly hand toward Vledder. Her eyes sparkled with humor.

"Well," she said laughingly, "you *are* a good looking man. I didn't know they picked them for that."

With swaying hips she led them into the bar.

"Well, Vledder is really the result of a mistake," said DeKok with a straight face.

"Mistake?" asked Sylvia and Vledder looked at his mentor in surprise.

"Yes," continued DeKok unperturbed. "The State Police missed him. You know how they are. They pick all the tall, blond men and then place them at the borders in full dress uniform to check passports. Pure advertising."

"Stop it," protested Sylvia, "that's enough teasing. How about a beer? I have to check the pressure anyway, I just hooked up a new barrel."

She moved behind the counter and busied herself with the tap and three glasses. Vledder and DeKok hoisted themselves on barstools. It was dark in the room. Only the lights over the bar were lit. DeKok leaned forward.

"How long have we known each other, Sylvia?"

She cocked her head at him enticingly, a bit mocking but with a certain hint of affection.

"Fifteen years, sixteen, maybe. Why? Are you going to propose?"

DeKok smiled.

"No," he said simply, "but I did want you to know that I have you more or less figured out. I think I know what makes you tick."

Her look became suspicious.

"What *are* you driving at?"

DeKok's face became serious.

"What sort of papers did Jacques have with him?"

Without looking at the gray sleuth, she placed a beer in front of him. Her hand shook slightly.

"Jacques ... Jacques had no papers."

"But you looked?"

She nodded slowly.

"But not to steal."

DeKok rubbed his face with a tired hand.

"I know that, Sylvia." His tone was friendly, almost fatherly. "That's a long time ago. These days you only look because you're curious."

She reacted vehemently.

"I'm entitled to know who I take in. He could have been dangerous, escaped from an institution, or something."

"Relax," soothed DeKok, "I understand. But Jacques had no papers of any kind?"

She shook her head.

"No, nothing. Nothing at all. No letters, no passport, no wallet... nothing. Not even a picture of any kind, no woman, no child ... nothing. I never encountered anything like it before. Usually there is at least *something*."

DeKok took a swallow from his beer. He preferred cognac.

"What happened to the clothes he was wearing . . . the clothes he had when you met him?"

She gestured toward the outside.

"I threw them away."

"Did you look where they had been bought? I mean, was there a label from a department store, or a tailor?"

She shrugged her shoulders.

"I didn't notice, didn't look for it. I told you: just a bunch of rags. Too far gone, even for the Salvation Army."

DeKok drummed his fingers on top of the bar.

"Wasn't there anything at all?" His voice sounded irritated. "Darn it, we've been on the case for three days and we *still* don't know who he is."

Thoughtfully she bit her lower lip. It made her look charming, almost child-like.

"I have a draft . . ."

DeKok looked at her with astonishment in his eyes.

"A draft?"

"Yes, well, a scribble really, a draft for a letter, the beginning of a letter."

DeKok looked at her angrily, a bit hurt.

"Why didn't you say so before?"

She pouted like a child.

"You never asked," she said accusingly. "Anyway, it's nothing, DeKok, believe me. Just a crumpled piece of paper. That's all. Just a few lines. I found it in the waste basket one morning. It was all balled up. I think Jacques may have been writing upstairs while I was down here, in the bar."

"When was that?"

"The night that he left."

"Where is it?"

"Upstairs."

She took a key from a pocket and came from behind the bar.

"Just wait a moment," she said, "I'll go get it. I'll be right back."

She almost ran to the stairs at the end of the room. Like so many bars in the Quarter, if the upstairs was not used as an informal brothel, it would generally serve as living quarters for the owner. The two inspectors watched her leave with silent admiration for the shapeliness of her legs and returned their attentions to their beers.

It took a few minutes. Then she returned, waving a piece of paper over her head. Panting, she hoisted herself on a barstool next to DeKok and smoothed the piece of paper on the counter top.

"Here . . . you see, nothing special. Just a rough draft. A bit strange, maybe, but it's only the beginning of something."

DeKok leaned closer to the piece of paper. He noticed a smoothly flowing handwriting with clear, easy to read words. Slowly he read it to himself:

Amice, I've reached the end of my odyssey. I have found her and you know what that means. It's strange, but I'm neither happy, nor bitter. My heart is empty. There are even moments that I doubt myself, feel unable to proceed with my plan. Sometimes it all seems so senseless. But whatever happens . . .

The letter ended there. It was neither dated, nor addressed. Was not finished and not signed. For one reason or another, the writer had suddenly stopped, balled up the piece of paper and tossed it carelessly aside. Slowly DeKok raised his gaze until he looked Sylvia in the eyes. There was a searching look in his eyes.

"Why did you keep it so carefully?"

She smiled a sad smile.

"Because I'm a sentimental fool." It sounded like an apology. "The men in my life never leave much behind. Some I can remember hardly at all." She made a vague gesture. "I didn't want Jacques to disappear that completely, you see. That's why I kept it . . . as a sort of souvenir. Apart from my memories, it's all I have left of him."

DeKok rubbed the bridge of his nose with a little finger.

"Are you sure, Sylvia, that *sentiment* is the only reason?" There was a hint of suspicion in his voice.

She did not answer at once. Her dark eyes sparkled. She looked evenly at him, challenging, defiant.

"What other reason could I have, DeKok?"

* * *

With his hands deep in the pockets of his trousers, DeKok paced up and down between the desks in the large detective room in Warmoes Street Station. Most of the desks were deserted. Here and there a policeman was quietly working on some paperwork, a phone rang from time to time and there was the occasional clatter of Vledder's computer terminal.

DeKok's face was glum. The pacing did nothing to help order his thoughts. Everything was so vague, leads disappeared into nowhere. The case started to bother him. It was a mess. After three days he had not progressed at all and he felt that he was getting further and further from the solution. It irritated him and it hurt him. As usual, whenever a case did not seem to progress, when he appeared to be searching in the dark, groping for a solution, a thousand invisible devils seemed to attack his lower extremities. He felt a thousand needles going through his calves and his feet were tired.

Laboriously he walked over to his desk and seated himself gingerly. With a sigh of relief he raised his feet and placed them on top of a pulled out drawer. He looked toward Vledder at the desk next to his.

"Did you reach the press?"

"Yes, I reached them all. They promised to do it up right."

"Excellent, really excellent. What about the police in St. Etienne?"

Vledder nodded.

"They promised to look it up for me. As soon as they know anything, they'll call back."

"Who did you talk to?"

"An Inspector Boulangier."

DeKok grimaced.

"Well, let's hope he'll be able to whip up some tasty bits of information."

Vledder laughed. He knew the symptoms of DeKok's painful feet and was glad his old friend was able to joke, however feeble the attempt.

"Over the phone he seemed like a nice enough guy, quite competent," said Vledder. "I told him I would be here until ten tonight and I gave him my home phone. If he doesn't call tonight, he will call tomorrow, regardless."

DeKok nodded approval.

"What's your opinion of the letter?"

Vledder shrugged his shoulders.

"It fits with what Uncle Steven told us about Marcel's alleged search for a cousin."

DeKok shook his head vehemently.

"It doesn't fit at all," he said sharply. "Not at all, at all."

Vledder looked at him with surprise.

"But why not?"

"Marcel wrote the letter when he was leaving Sylvia. That was *before* his departure from *The Blue Pitcher*. Now do you understand? The tale he told about his cousin, doesn't fit in with the letter."

Vledder's eyes gleamed with sudden understanding.

"You're right," he exclaimed with his sudden, exuberant enthusiasm. "In the letter it said that he had found her, but he told Uncle Steven he was still looking for her."

"Exactly. And there's something else that bothers me."

"Something else?"

DeKok nodded.

"Who is 'Amice'? For whom was the letter intended?"

9

A chilly, cold wind blew unimpeded through the bare shrubs and trees that surrounded St. Barbara's Cemetery. The sky was gray, threatening. A few blackbirds sought shelter behind a weathered grave stone where a kind hand had spread some seeds. From time to time, when a train passed on the nearby overpass they would briefly flare out in a confused kaleidoscope of black against gray and white marble. An aged funeral attendant, in long tails, gray gloves and a top hat shuffled from one group of visitors to another, a pen in one hand and a condolence book in the other.

DeKok kept himself in the background. He had pulled up the collar of his coat and pushed his hat far down over his eyes. Alertly he studied the slowly increasing group of visitors. He recognized Robert Hoveneer from a distance. He was accompanied by an attractive young woman and a distinguished looking gentleman in his early forties. DeKok guessed they were Uncle Charles and his young wife. Idly he made a note to himself to have a long, hearty conversation with Charles Hoveneer about his interest in Marcel's belongings. No doubt, he reflected, the shrewd broker would have a plausible explanation for his actions, otherwise he would hardly have attended the funeral of the victim this openly. All in all, it *was* rather strange that the wealthy Hoveneer family would show such interest in the funeral of a "tramp".

DeKok's sharp gaze traveled over the assembled visitors. A little off to one side he discovered Vledder's group of friendly reporters and to the left of them the group of old men and women that seemed to attend every funeral, driven by a ghoulish desire for sensation and misplaced excitement. DeKok hated the faces full of cruel curiosity. At one time he had taken the group aside and talked to them. It had become a sharp, malicious speech in which he had told them in no uncertain terms what he thought about their morbid curiosity. It gained him an official complaint for insulting the public and a chastising from the Judge-Advocate. Since that time he limited himself to uttering inaudible curses with a disapproving look on his face. But he left the macabre group alone, tried to ignore them.

The undertaker approached him across the gravel, made a polite little bow and held up the visitors book.

"You're here for the funeral of the unknown?" he lisped.

DeKok nodded and placed his signature in the book.

"In that case you're invited to a short ceremony in the Chapel, prior to internment," lisped the man.

DeKok looked at him in sudden surprise.

"A ceremony? I thought he was being buried from public funds?"

The other nodded.

"That was the intention," he lisped again, in the affected tone of a professional mourner. "But that changed at the last moment. A sponsor stepped forth."

"Oh? Who?"

The man hesitated.

"I ... I'm not allowed to say."

DeKok pushed his hat back and spread his legs a little further, assuming a solid, almost threatening stance.

"And why not, my friend?"

"The ... the sponsor expressly wished to remain anonymous."

The pale face of the undertaker showed a light blush. He felt trapped and tried to escape from DeKok's questions.

The inspector took him by one arm and felt for his badge with his free hand.

"My name is DeKok, DeKok with ... eh, kay-oh-kay. I'm in charge of the investigation regarding your unknown corpse."

The undertaker pursed his thin lips. He quickly regained his self-control.

"Aaaah," he said in a tone that seemed to explain everything. "Ah, well, yes. Yes, I can see how that makes a difference. After all, I couldn't tell you were a policeman, just by looking at you. Yes, I must tell you, if you're a representative of the Law."

DeKok grinned broadly.

"That I am, my friend, that I am. As far as looking like a policeman is concerned, that has nothing to do with the Law."

"Yes, of course, I can see that." The man smiled as if it hurt him to do so. He pulled off his gloves and picked a form from between the pages of the register.

"Here you are," he said resignedly. "Look for yourself. The sponsor is a Miss Mabel Paddington."

* * *

DeKok leaned against the oak wainscotting. The light in the Chapel was diffused. The stained-glass windows added their own colors to the flowers on the coffin. The turn-out was quite large, considering the dead man was unknown, apparently without friends, or family. Almost all chairs were occupied.

DeKok looked for Mabel Paddington. He did not see her. But he did discover Black Sylvia in one of the rear rows. She looked nervous and worried a minuscule handkerchief between her shaking hands. Next to her, ill at ease in a modern, dark-blue suit, sat Martin Kerkhoven, better known as the Slippery Eel. He wore a black band around his left arm.

A funeral attendant emerged from one of the side doors, carrying an easel. The man placed the easel to the side of the coffin. A second man emerged with a large, unframed painting, covered by a black cloth. The second man placed the painting on the easel, leaving it covered. Carefully he adjusted the easel to make sure that the sunlight would fall full on the painting when it was revealed.

DeKok watched the proceedings with mounting surprise. He was not the only one.

After the undertakers had left, soft organ music sounded through the small Chapel. A balding minister approached the lectern with short, slow steps. The music died away and the minister began to speak in soft, unctuous tones. He spoke about the paradox of short love affairs that lasted an eternity ... about the departed loved one, who knew his murderer ... about justice, if not of this earth, most surely in Heaven. After about ten minutes he finished with a pathetic cry:

"His blood will be upon us and our children ..."

DeKok thought it a confusing and confused speech. He was again surprised when Mabel Paddington next appeared from the side door. She wore a long, ankle length, black dress. She approached the coffin and took her place between the minister and the painting.

The organ started again.

DeKok watched the young woman carefully. She seemed changed to him. In the few days since he had first met her, she seemed to have lost weight. Her face looked gaunt. She was as pale as transparent alabaster and there was a strange, feverish light in her eyes. He wondered what drove her. Hate, jealousy, remorse? Had she directed this strange scenario in the Chapel? Was it all her plan? But why? What was the purpose of the covered painting, next to the coffin?

When the last tones of the organ had ebbed away, a strange expectant, almost fearful, silence fell on the congregation. Encased in her severe black dress, the hair combed straight on either side of her face, Mabel Paddington had remained motionless throughout. In the dim light of the Chapel her face seemed to glow from within, an oval white spot with an eery light that caught everybody's attention.

In response to a signal from the minister, she leaned over toward the painting and suddenly jerked the black cover from the canvas.

DeKok froze momentarily and a shrill cry sounded from one of the forward benches. Exactly in the center of two light beams from opposing windows a lugubrious painting was revealed: an insistent death-mask with the unmistakable expression of the deceased. A realistic, gaping wound was painted on the forehead. Fresh blood seemed to drip from the wound.

DeKok came into action before the uproar subsided. He quickly walked over to Mabel Paddington who seemed ready to faint. He took the young woman by the arm and led her to an adjoining room. From the door he looked back. Robert and Charles Hoveneer were bent over a motionless figure. Mrs. Hoveneer had fainted.

* * *

DeKok held Mabel by both arms and shook her roughly.

"Whatever came over you?" he cried angrily. "Have you gone nuts? Who's that crazy minister?"

She looked at him as if drugged.

"Did you make that terrible painting?" he asked.

"Yes."

"Who's that minister?'

"He isn't a minister."

"Who is he?"

"An actor."

DeKok shook his head in despair.

"What's his connection to all this?"

"Nothing. I hired him."

"Hired him? Why?"

She looked at him with glowing eyes.

"You let Robert go."

DeKok nodded.

"I found no proof of guilt, nothing that would stick."

Sadly she shook her head.

"And I thought you were a competent police officer."

* * *

Leaning back in his chair, his legs stretched out comfortably in front of him, DeKok told the strange story of the funeral.

Young Vledder listened intently.

"So," he said, "as I understand it, Mabel only paid for the funeral in order to be able to perform this strange charade in the Chapel?"

"Exactly."

"But why? What did she hope to gain?"

"She was trying to shock the killer."

"What?"

"Yes, it took her a single night to paint that horrible painting and she hoped to scare the killer, bring him out into the open. When she discussed the plan with a friend at the Art Academy, the friend suggested the dramatic unveiling. The friend, a girl with a real morbid sense of reality, apparently, also knew an actor who would play the role of minister."

Vledder shook his head in bemusement.

"But how did they pull it off? I mean, how did they get the undertaker crazy enough that he would cooperate?"

DeKok gestured.

"Mabel misled him. When she discussed the preparations with the undertaker, she showed him a regular painting of Marcel that she had painted some time ago. I've seen it, it's really well done. Of course the undertaker did not object that *that* painting would be displayed. Then, this morning, while the undertaker was otherwise occupied and his assistants weren't looking, she exchanged the paintings."

"And ... did it work?"

"How do you mean?"

"Did the killer reveal himself?"

DeKok shook his head impatiently.

"Robert Hoveneer reacted hardly at all."

The young inspector looked at DeKok with a confused look on his face.

"You said: *Robert* Hoveneer?"

DeKok nodded.

"According to Mabel, there's no doubt. Robert is the killer."

They remained silent for a long while. The riddles surrounding the mysterious death occupied their thoughts. Vledder was the first to break the silence.

"Where are the paintings now?" he asked.

DeKok gestured with his thumb.

"Downstairs, in the evidence room. I felt it better to relieve her of the paintings, for the time being. I was afraid she might use them for some other crazy stunt. In her present state of mind, I think she may be capable of anything."

He paused and scratched the back of his neck. Gloomily he stared into the distance.

"I advised her," he continued after another long silence, "to stay with a friend for the time being. She certainly has to be away from that house on the Emperor's Canal. The continuing confrontations with Robert could lead to all sorts of obsessions. You never know what might happen."

Vledder nodded absent-mindedly. It seemed as if he listened with only half an ear. Then he said:

"May I see those paintings?"

"Of course, let's go."

They left the detective room and descended down to the basement. In a dark, windowless room they found the most unusual collection of strange, unconnected items imaginable. All the items, at one time or another, had figured as "evidence" in some case. DeKok picked up the paintings and placed them on a table under a dim overhead light. Again he was impressed by the warm, lifelike portrait and he shivered at the sight of the dreadful death-mask.

"Terrible, don't you think?"

Vledder did not answer at once. He bit his lower lip in thought.

"You're right," he said after a while. "It's enough to give you nightmares." He lifted the painting from the table and held it at an angle.

"Did you show her Marcel, after he was dead?" asked Vledder.

DeKok shook his head.

"She wanted to see him. She was angry when I refused. But it really wasn't necessary. The first painting was enough proof of identification for my purposes."

Vledder nodded his understanding.

"Did you tell her what he looked like?"

Distracted, DcKok looked up.

"No," he answered slowly, "I didn't. When she insisted, I told her that it was better if she remembered him whole, unblemished."

"Did you mention the wound?"

"I tried to tell her that it was for her own peace of mind, her own good, if she didn't see Marcel anymore, because he had a terrible injury on the head."

"That's all?"

"Yes, that's all."

DeKok stared at his young colleague with a mixture of approval and wonder. His mind tried to fathom the sudden spate of questions, but more than that, he tried to figure out what had led Vledder on this particular line of questioning. His gaze went again to the abhorrent painting and suddenly he gave Vledder a thundering clap on the shoulder.

"Well done, Dick," he exclaimed. "You're right. You're absolutely one hundred percent right. The wound in the painting is exactly the right size and is exactly in the same place."

Vledder grinned without mirth.

"Mabel Paddington is either clairvoyant ... or she knew exactly where and how to paint the injury."

10

Inspector DeKok left the tiny restaurant of his good friend Tjong Hong Sie with a satisfied smile on his face and an excess of Tjong's excellent Chinese food in his stomach. He just couldn't help himself. He seldom indulged in Chinese food for that very reason. Whenever he did, he invariably ate too much.

He consoled himself and soothed his conscience with the thought that he would walk it off. Leisurely he strolled along the canals and through the alleys of the Quarter until he reached the station house.

When he entered the detective room he found Vledder studying the newspapers. With a smile, the younger man looked up.

"Have you seen the evening papers?"

DeKok shook his head.

"My friend, the all-wise Tjong Hong Sie, bans all newspapers and any other form of news from his establishment. If you enter with a paper, you're asked to surrender it, or he won't feed you."

"Surrender?"

DeKok grinned broadly.

"Mister Tjong is of the opinion that the taste of his dishes should not be spoiled by bad news."

Vledder unfolded one of the papers.

"Well," he said, "this wouldn't have spoiled your appetite. Almost half a page about the funeral this morning. The press really played it up. They went into great detail about that bizarre performance in the Chapel and Mr. Charles Hoveneer is very, very angry."

DeKok looked up.

"Angry? How do you know?"

Vledder pointed at the telephone.

"While you were overindulging in Chinese culinary delights, the phone hasn't stopped. A string of reporters told me, more or less gleefully, that Mr. Charles Hoveneer has filed a complaint. He feels highly insulted because his name has been featured so prominently in the articles. Words like libel have been bandied about."

DeKok seated himself behind his desk.

"And furthermore," continued his colleague, "Mabel Paddington has disappeared without a trace."

"What!?"

"Exactly what I said: disappeared, without a trace. One of the reporters told me and another confirmed it. They wanted to know if we knew where she was. They wanted to interview her about the scene in the Chapel. But nobody can find her."

DeKok shrugged his shoulders.

"I can imagine that she hides from the reporters. They practically attacked her this morning. Your friends turned into a screaming mob of *paparazzi*. I had the greatest difficulty getting her into a cab."

He rubbed the bridge of his nose with a little finger. Vledder had never been able to figure out what that gesture meant. It happened often, but there was no way to predict when, where, or why DeKok felt compelled to make the gesture. DeKok had so many habits, some of them quite irritating.

"Any news from St. Etienne?" asked DeKok.

"Yes."

"And?"

Vledder shook his head.

"They don't know anything about a Marcel Duval," he said gravely. "That's to say, they know nothing about a Marcel Duval with a French father and a Dutch mother. They checked the town records and they checked with the churches. When they got no results that way, they put a description together and tried to get some results by asking around."

"Well?"

Vledder smiled.

"Inspector Boulangier of the St. Etienne police force took three minutes to express his regrets."

"In other words: not a clue!"

"No, we can safely forget the information from *The Blue Pitcher*. Our corpse did not originate in St. Etienne."

DeKok sighed.

"I was afraid of that."

He tried to find a more comfortable position in his chair. The abundant meal was still bothering him.

"Somebody," he said, "who grows up in France, even with a Dutch mother, always has some sort of accent when he speaks Dutch. Generally you can tell it's French. Just think of the Belgians. They're bilingual and normally half speak French and the rest speak Flemish, but when they speak each other's language, there's always an accent." He shook his head. "None of the witnesses mentioned an accent. Apparently Marcel spoke fluent Dutch."

Vledder appeared a bit confused.

"Then . . . you don't believe he came from France?"

DeKok smiled.

"Oh, he's undoubtedly *been* in France. But he was just another Dutchman, no more, no less. And that's why it's so frustrating that we still haven't been able to establish his identity. It's too absurd. I've *never* encountered such a case before. We're too small, the most densely populated country in the world, everything is registered, recorded, duplicated, filed away, cross-indexed and catalogued. It's nigh well impossible to disappear without *somebody* knowing about it, reporting it, or whatever. There are always parents, brothers, sisters, children, neighbors, acquaintances, colleagues, ad infinitum. Sooner or later somebody is going to the police to 'express his, or her, concern'. Even a misanthrope has social connections in Holland."

Vledder grinned.

"Yes, we may be the most tolerant country in the world, but that doesn't mean we're not nosy. Besides . . . our friend wasn't exactly a misanthrope."

DeKok drummed his fingers on the desk top.

"Exactly. That's why there have *got* to be people who know his identity." He rose from behind his desk and ambled over to the coat rack. "Did you ever wonder why nobody stepped forth?"

"No."

Abruptly DeKok turned and stretched out an index finger toward the younger man.

"Try it," he said.

Vledder shrugged his shoulders nonchalantly.

"Maybe . . . maybe," he said slowly, hesitating, "maybe nobody has missed him yet . . ."

DeKok grinned his friendly, infectious grin.

"Do you really believe," he said with a sarcastic tone in his voice, "that nobody woke up after all those reports in the papers? Come on, you don't believe that yourself!" He paused. "Let me tell you something," he continued, "the people who know him, who know the identity of our corpse, have something to gain by remaining silent." He got into his coat. "This case stinks . . . it stinks like the waters of the Brewers Canal from which we fished him."

His hat in his hand, he stood there for another moment, silent, thinking, a bitter expression around his lips.

"But," he said grimly, "if they think they can fool an old hand like me, they're wrong . . . dead wrong."

It sounded like a threat. He placed his hat firmly on top of his head and walked away with large steps.

"Where are you going?" called Vledder.

"Hoveneer," was the short answer.

Vledder grabbed his coat and ran after him.

* * *

The blonde girl, dressed in a maid's uniform, consisting of a tight-fitting black dress and a white apron, looked with surprise at the two men on the doorstep.

The gray sleuth lifted his hat in greeting.

"My name is DeKok, with kay-oh-kay. This is my colleague, Inspector Vledder. We're attached to the War-moes Street station."

"Inspectors?"

"Indeed. We would like to speak to Mr. Charles Hoveneer."

111

The girl made a gesture as if drying her hands with a slip of her apron.

"I'll tell him you're here then, shall I?"

When she turned to leave, DeKok restrained her by placing his hand lightly on her arm.

"How long have you worked here?"

She gave him a sweet smile.

"Just three days, is all."

"Do you live in?"

She swept her blonde hair from left to right in a gesture of denial.

"No, thank goodness. I just come in the morning for a few hours and again in the afternoon, is all. I'm home the rest of the time."

"Have you seen Miss Mabel, today?"

Her face fell.

"Miss Paddington has left. Mr. Charles don't know where she is, either. He's *that* worried about it. We're scared something might have happened."

"We?"

"Yes, Mrs. Hoveneer is worried too and young Mister Robert wanted . . ."

Charles Hoveneer entered the hall at that moment. His face was red with anger,

"What gives you the right to interrogate my personnel? I demand you leave immediately."

DeKok looked at him with an expression that combined tolerant amusement and a determined challenge.

"What gives you the right to prohibit me from interrogating anybody?"

Charles Hoveneer was dressed in a long robe. His feet were shod with suede slippers. He came nearer, suspicion in his eyes.

"Who are you?" he asked with a menacing tone.

"DeKok . . ."

" . . . with kay-oh-kay," completed Vledder.

The broker's face cleared.

"Ah, Mr. DeKok," he said cheerfully. "Is it really you? But come in, come in." He waved the maid away. "I had expected you sooner," he continued, turning his back on the two inspectors.

He led the way toward a large study. His manner was friendly and hospitable. DeKok looked at the rows upon rows of yellowed books that seemed to cover every spare area of wall space. Then he looked at his host who waved invitingly toward a few easy chairs.

"Please sit down, gentlemen. I'm sorry I took you for a couple of journalists." His tone was jovial, but Vledder and DeKok noted a forced quality to his joviality. "Really," continued their host, "they don't give us a moment's peace . . . They're downright rude. I would not have believed that such a thing was possible in Holland. Just because I refuse to give them an interview, they haunt my personnel and they write insinuating pieces. Did you see tonight's papers?"

He took a seat opposite the inspectors.

"I immediately filed a complaint with the Judge-Advocate, Mr. Overcinge. I simply do not care to have my name connected with the death of that unfortunate young man, whoever he may be."

DeKok sighed.

"Well, you have yourself to blame for that, more or less. You shouldn't have attended the funeral."

Mr. Hoveneer's face became red.

"But it was no more than an act of piety," he exclaimed. "That was all, no more. From Robert I understood the man had visited my home several times. Without my knowing

113

about it, needless to say, but that's neither here nor there. In view of the relationship between the deceased and Mabel I felt obliged to show an interest."

He made an uncontrolled gesture.

"How was I to know that Mabel would create such a . . . a spectacle? It was downright embarrassing." He shook his head. "And then the crazy speech from that half-drunk . . . actor . . . really, it was too terrible for words."

A woman entered the study through the hall-door. She was tall, slender and extremely beautiful. DeKok estimated her to be in her late twenties. When she came nearer he realized that her age was difficult, if not impossible to define. Her remarkable beauty was rigid, sterile and nearly timeless. The blonde hair that fell in long waves around both shoulders, reminded him of Brunhilde, the blonde heroine of the Niebelungen.

Charles Hoveneer rose immediately from his seat and walked toward her.

"Two gentlemen from the police, my dear. The famous Inspector DeKok and his assistant . . ." He looked a question at the young inspector.

"Vledder."

The broker smiled.

"Vledder," he continued. "I already told them that we were extremely shocked by Mabel's incredible performance in the Chapel this morning and that we would never have permitted Mabel to . . ."

Mrs. Hoveneer shook a cool hand with the inspectors and sat down. Outwardly she was calm, controlled, completely self-possessed. She crossed her long legs and immediately began to speak.

"Mabel," she said softly, apologetically, "is an emotional young woman. She has a hard time dealing with the loss of her young friend. It will, I think, take a long time before she will be able to accept his death as final. For several days she's been behaving rather erratically. I think you must see her flight in that light."

DeKok looked at her quizzically.

"Flight?"

She sighed deeply and closed her eyes.

"Mabel has fled."

The gray inspector continued to look at her, searchingly.

"Fled? From whom? From what?"

She reacted in an irritated manner. The cool veneer slightly marred by DeKok's tone.

"Don't you understand? This house has too many memories for her. It was impossible for her to remain here any longer. She would have gone mad. She already suffered from hallucinations."

"Such as?"

Mrs. Hoveneer avoided his gaze.

"She suspects Robert. She thinks *he's* responsible for the death of her friend."

"Why?"

"Out of jealousy. But that's ridiculous. Robert is a dear boy. He's been in this house for a long time. He wouldn't harm a fly."

Charles Hoveneer nodded agreement.

"It hurt us," he said, "that Robert should have been accused of murder. You can see that. We've tried to talk her out of this . . . this obsession, but one way or the other she remains convinced."

"Proof?"

Mrs. Hoveneer's mouth formed a pitying smile that did not reach her eyes.

"A woman in love doesn't require proof. She knows . . . she feels."

Vledder grinned.

"Feelings," he said contemptuously, "what are feelings? There isn't a judge in the world that will accept that in a court of law."

Charles Hoveneer waved a hand in a vague gesture, as if dismissing the possibility.

"It's not to be contemplated." His tone was shocked, indignant. "Robert is innocent. It's extremely unkind that Mabel should accuse him, should look upon him as a murderer. As soon as she returns, I'll insist that she apologizes."

DeKok's eyebrows seemed to contract, as if ready to spring forth. Then they relaxed. Only Vledder, always on the alert for such manifestations, had noticed. DeKok looked at the face of the broker and wondered if the man was joking. But the face of Hoveneer showed only righteous indignation. He was completely serious.

DeKok leaned forward in his chair.

"Did you know the deceased?" he asked.

"No."

"You never met him in the house?"

Hoveneer shook his head.

"I think that Mabel took care to keep him out of sight of the family circle."

DeKok nodded.

"That's possible," he answered slowly. "When did you first hear about him?"

The broker remained silent. Thoughtfully he stared into the middle distance. Then he looked at DeKok.

"About three weeks, ago," he said. "I think that's when Robert mentioned something about a man who visited Mabel in her room."

"What did you do then?"

"Nothing. It was one of the consequences of having taken her in. Alice warned me, when Mabel's parents asked if she could stay with us. She tried to dissuade me. Young girls are a lot of trouble, she said." He smiled wanly. "Of course, I had no way of knowing that the troubles would grow out of proportion to the extent they have."

"So, you did not call Mabel to account?"

"No, I judged it senseless. She's supposed to be old and wise enough to know her own mind. It's certainly not up to me to try and correct her behavior at this late date."

DeKok looked at him sharply.

"You didn't approach the man, either?"

Hoveneer seemed confused.

"Really," he exclaimed. "If I didn't confront Mabel, why should I speak to the man? The man didn't interest me in the least."

This time all noticed the sudden dance of DeKok's eyebrows. The Hoveneers seemed momentarily stunned, Vledder smiled. Just as sudden as the eyebrows had come into violent motion, they subsided.

"That's weird." remarked DeKok casually.

"What is?"

"Why did you go to *The Blue Pitcher*, the day after the murder and why did you try to obtain the possessions of the deceased?"

11

Silently the two inspectors left the Emperor's Canal and turned off into a side street. Their thoughts still dwelled on the interview with Charles Hoveneer.

"What did you think about his explanations?" asked Vledder.

DeKok pushed his lower lip forward.

"Ingenious, to say the least. It would not at all have been outside the realms of possibilities if Mabel had written her Marcel a number of foolish letters. Not impossible at all, at all. In that case it would be logical that Charles, fearing eventual blackmail, would try to get the letters back. You can hardly blame him for that. It's the sort of thing you'd expect from a wise old uncle with a lot of experience with people."

Vledder shook his head, grinning.

"It's a fairy-tale. Mabel never wrote him. She didn't even know the address. You asked her yourself. She had never *heard* of The Blue Pitcher." He looked at DeKok. "Besides," he added thoughtfully, "who was supposed to do the alleged blackmail? Marcel was already dead."

The gray sleuth ignored the remarks with his usual sublime indifference. Vledder, who was used to DeKok's peculiarities, took no offense.

Silently they walked on, both occupied with their own thoughts. Suddenly Vledder nudged DeKok's elbow.

"I just had another thought about the motives of Uncle Charles."

"So?"

"Yes, Uncle Charles wasn't worried about possible blackmail of Mabel. He was afraid that Marcel had papers that could incriminate Charles himself."

"What sort of papers?"

"How should I know," exclaimed Vledder, slightly irritated. "I just don't like Mister Charles Hoveneer. He's too friendly, too slippery. I think he's a lot closer connected to the murder than we can possibly suspect at this time. Have you considered that the burglar only used Mabel's feelings, her affection for him, in order to gain easy access to the house?"

DeKok looked at him from under the brim of his ridiculous little felt hat.

"Sometimes," he said in a friendly tone of voice, "you can say remarkably intelligent things."

This time it was Vledder who did not react to the other's remarks. But he tasted the words of his mentor, mulled them over in his head and wondered how to take them, how to interpret them.

"But the question remains," said the young man after a considerable pause, "what was it that Marcel was seeking in the house on the Emperor's Canal? What was he after? Money, jewelry, papers?"

DeKok shook his head.

"If that was Marcel's objective, he'd have been better off to stick to the Slippery Eel. No ... despite the burglary clothes, I don't think that his killing had anything to do with a break-in. There are other motives, different forces, at work here. There are too many things we don't yet know."

* * *

Corporal Dompeler, the acting Watch Commander, looked startled when Vledder and DeKok entered the station.

"Where *were* you guys?" He almost stuttered with indignation. "I know you don't like walkie-talkies, DeKok, but you could let Vledder wear one. And you were walking again, I bet. Your car didn't respond either. I even sent a cruiser through the neighborhood, looking for you."

DeKok pushed his hat back on his head.

"So, what's so important, all of a sudden?"

"There are two people waiting for you. Uncle Steven Blader and one of his guests. They told me it was very important. They seemed to think it has something to do with your mysterious corpse."

"Where did you put them?"

"In the waiting room. I thought it better to hold on to them for a while."

The waiting room in Dutch police stations is a peculiar facility. It is indeed a room where people wait. People in the waiting room are not, technically, under arrest. But nobody ever leaves without official permission. One can smoke, drink, eat, even play cards in the waiting room, but one has to wait, nevertheless.

"Thanks," winked DeKok as those thoughts flashed through his mind. He did not think there was an equivalent for the waiting room on any other police force in the world.

Uncle Steven pointed at a bashful old man in a wrinkled, black suit. His head was crowned with a long, silvery mane and his face looked like the blushing face of an apple-cheeked cherubim.

"This is Uncle Lewis."

Vledder looked at the man. Why, he thought to himself, are all old men and women in Holland automatically promoted to the rank of "Uncle", or "Aunt"?

The cherubim bowed politely, oblivious to Vledder's thoughts.

"Uncle Lewis," continued the hotel-keeper, "Is one of my regulars. He's just back from a short stint in the Municipal Correction Facility. Nothing major, you understand, just a few tickets. Uncle Lewis sells pornography without a license."

DeKok grimaced.

"At least he supplies a demand."

The hotel-keeper grinned. Vledder, who was more and more getting used to DeKok's tolerant views of minor misdemeanors and peccadilloes, smiled agreeably.

"Anyways," continued Uncle Steven, "I told Uncle Lewis that you had been around, yesterday, for information and that Marcel was dead. That they killed him." He gestured toward the small, old man. "Well, then *he* said that it wasn't a big surprise, that he had more or less expected it."

DeKok's eyes widened fractionally.

"That's interesting," he commented.

Uncle Steven nodded agreement with a serious face.

"I thought so too. So I told Uncle here that if he had something important, he was to tell you about it. So I brought him over. You see, they shared a room for a while, Uncle Lewis and Marcel. And Marcel must have said something, then." Again he pointed in the direction of the cherubic figure. "Maybe Uncle Lewis should tell you himself."

DeKok nodded.

The little old man took a few diffident paces forward. "Marcel was a learned person," he said with conviction. "A fine person. He didn't belong in our boarding house. He was too much of a gentleman for that. I told him so, once, when there was just the two of us. He laughed, a bit sadly, I think, and said that he had expected his life to be different."

Vledder pushed a chair closer and urged the small, fragile looking man to sit down. The old man sat down with a smile of thanks on his lips. He folded his hands on his stomach.

"I'm from a good background myself, sir, although you wouldn't say so now, when you look at me."

DeKok nodded encouragement.

"I noticed that at once," he lied.

Uncle Lewis beamed.

"Yes, background will not be denied. A good upbringing is a blessing."

Again DeKok nodded agreement.

"You were going to tell us about Marcel."

The little man moved in his chair, as if looking for a soft spot on the hard, institutionalized piece of furniture.

"Yes, Marcel. Well, as I said, we happened to be together that night. I still had a few bottles of beer underneath my bed and we drank some. I told him about my own life, that I had hoped, in the past, to do a lot better than I wound up doing. Let's be frank, what am I, after all? A somewhat disreputable distributor of naughty literature." He remained silent for a while, rubbing idly at one of the many spots on his waistcoat. "Anyway," he continued, "you know how it goes when two men have a few drinks together.

Especially us northerners. Eventually we become solemn, melancholy and start confiding things."

"Then what?"

The cherubim sighed.

"After a while Marcel told me that he, too, had come to the end of his career. I laughed at him and told him he was much too young to talk about an end of his career. He had his whole life before him, after all. That's what I said. Then he shook his head and told me that it wouldn't be long before he would die for real."

DeKok looked up sharply.

"*What* did he say?"

The little man made a vague gesture.

"Marcel seemed to be convinced that he wasn't going to be much longer for this world. The strange thing was, that it didn't seem to bother him. He spoke quite naturally about it. One way or the other, he said, there's an end to everything. He didn't mind dying. He gave the impression of being deeply disillusioned, you understand, as if life had lost all flavor."

DeKok rubbed his gray hair.

"What was he doing in Amsterdam?" he asked. "He didn't belong here, did he?"

Uncle Lewis shrugged his shoulders.

"He talked about a mission that had to be completed, but he didn't seem to believe in it anymore."

"What sort of mission?"

"I don't know. He was a bit vague about that. Evil will be punished, he used to say. Evil is its own reward, no sin remains unpunished, words to that effect. It was a bit muddled, I thought. At one point he said something like: Justice is the result of fate and not the task of people. I'm sure that's what he said."

DeKok pushed his lower lip forward, an approving look on his face.

"A nice slogan," he admired.

The little man nodded slowly.

"I told you, Marcel was a learned man. He said more striking things that night, profound things, but I can't remember them all. You ask Steven. After I've had a few, my mind becomes a sieve. Nothing lasts. One time . . ."

DeKok waved the new story aside.

"Did he say anything about a cousin he was looking for?"

Uncle Lewis stared in the distance, obviously trying to remember.

"No," he said after a long pause. "No, I don't think so. At least, I don't remember."

"What about a house on the Emperor's Canal?"

Uncle Lewis shook his head. He seemed genuinely disappointed to be of so little help.

"There's one thing I *do* remember," he said after a while. "That's his name."

DeKok looked more cheerful.

"His name?" he asked brightly.

"Yes, he was in bed already and I was still puttering around. Suddenly he sat up and said: If something ever happens to me, Uncle Lewis, go to the police and tell them my name is Tjeerd Talema."

"Tjeerd Talema?"

The old man nodded emphatically.

"Yes, from Friesland, you know."

"You don't have to tell me that. I recognize a Frisian name when I hear it."

"Well, yes, of course you do. But Marcel wasn't his real name. He just used that name because he didn't want anyone to know that his real name was Tjeerd Talema."

"And why was that."

Uncle Lewis made a sad gesture.

"I don't know that either. Maybe he told me and maybe he didn't. I just don't remember. I was a bit tipsy, you know. One beer too many." He sighed. "I only remembered the name because he mentioned it again the next day. Then I was stone cold sober."

DeKok swallowed his impatience.

"He mentioned it again?"

Uncle Lewis nodded.

"Next day he was waiting for me at the front door. He seemed a bit confused. What did I tell you last night? he asked. I shrugged my shoulders. Nothing special, I answered. We had a few beers, maybe one too many. He looked at me for a long time, strangely, with a suspicious look in his eyes. Did I mention the name Tjeerd Talema, he asked. I think so, I said, carelessly, you know, as if it wasn't all that important. I understood that he regretted his confidence, that he had said too much."

"Then what?"

"He hesitated for a while. Seemed to be looking for words. Of course, he was wondering how much I knew, how much he had said. Maybe he didn't remember exactly what he had said himself. Forget it, he said after a while. Forget everything, he repeated. When I've been drinking I say the craziest things, he added. I laughed at him. Did you say something? I asked, surprised-like, you know. I wanted to make sure he knew that I had forgotten it already."

Uncle Lewis remained silent. Then he gave DeKok a dreamy look.

"And I *would* have forgotten it," he said after a long pause, "if Uncle Steven hadn't told me that Marcel had been murdered. That's when I remembered the name Tjeerd Talema and some parts of the conversation we had that night."

He rubbed his eyes with a tired gesture.

"I sincerely hope you will find the killer, Mr. DeKok. Not because I believe in justice, but because I found Marcel, whatever his name was, a fine person, a good human being."

DeKok looked at him.

There was a tear on the cheek of the cherubim.

12

Commissaris Buitendam did not seem to fit in the hustle and bustle of the busy Warmoes Street station. He was tall and stately and looked more like a retired diplomat than the chief of the busiest police station in Northern Europe. With a gesture of barely controlled anger he tossed his pen on the desk. His usually pale cheeks were spotted with bright blushes of excitement.

"The Judge-Advocate," he said in his affected, frog-in-throat voice, "Mr. Overcinge, has asked me for information. He has received an official complaint from a certain Hoveneer. And I knew nothing ... nothing about what's going on. I was forced to get my information from the newspapers."

DeKok laughed happily, completely uninhibited.

"It was a very good report," he said.

The Commissaris shook his head violently.

"That's hardly the issue," he exclaimed. "I want to know what's happening. I have a right to know what's happening. In case you had forgotten, you're supposed to be working under my supervision, in accordance with my directions."

He stretched an arm toward DeKok in a threatening gesture. "And I warn you, DeKok, despite your many qualities as a detective, your many services to the department, if you ever hide something from me again . . ."

The gray sleuth looked at him in genuine surprise. He ignored the veiled threat, his position was secure. He had too much seniority and was too valuable. It would probably take an act of Congress to get him fired at this stage in his career. At the same time he philosophically realized that he would never be promoted again. He would eventually retire with the rank of Inspector. All that did not bother him at all. No, he was genuinely upset by the thought that the Commissaris would think that he was hiding things.

"Hiding?" he said, indignation in his voice, "but it was in all the papers."

The commissarial face became redder still.

"You know very well what I mean, DeKok." Again he gestured wildly with an outstretched arm. "Who is Hoveneer?"

"A broker. A man well known in stock market circles. He enjoys, I believe, a certain notoriety, or is it fame? I never know the difference."

"What does he have to do with the murder?'

DeKok shrugged his shoulders, oblivious to the fact that he was infuriating his chief even more.

"I don't know," he said while he gave the tall, stately man an open and frank look. "But I would like to ask him."

Suiting his actions to his words, he stood up and walked toward the door.

The Commissaris called him back. Shaking with anger the man supported himself on the edge of his desk.

"I want a report from you within the hour."

"I have, as yet, nothing to report. There's no sensible word to say about the entire case."

"I . . . want . . . a . . . report!"

Again DeKok walked toward the door.

"Very well, sir," he said in parting, "I'll see what I can do about it."

His tone should have warned the Commissaris. DeKok was, in many ways, a law onto himself. He hated and despised the rules, regulations and red-tape that hampered so much of true police work. He knew from experience that every word that was ever written down, was capable of haunting him for the rest of his days. That was one of the main reasons he did not indulge in interim reports. Interim reports, according to DeKok, were time-wasters, busy work for a bunch of clerks with nothing better to do than to check the spelling and grammar of hard-working policemen. But the Commissaris was too angry to realize that.

He should have, but his character always made him forget. It was against his nature. Every day the Commissaris read hundreds of reports from the men and women attached to his station. Neatly typed in triplicate in the required folders, attached to the necessary routing slips. That was order, that was regulation, that was expected. But not DeKok. If it had not been for Vledder, the Commissaris might never know about some of the spectacular cases that DeKok solved with seemingly uncanny ease. The Commissaris knew for a fact that DeKok had never even used his computer terminal. It was shoved to the side of his desk and might occasionally be used as a resting place for DeKok's ridiculous, little hat.

Suddenly DeKok reappeared in the room. A crumpled piece of paper protruded from his large hand. He approached the desk and handed the piece of paper to the Commissaris.

"Here's your report."

The police chief looked suspiciously at the outstretched hand.

"That was quick."

DeKok nodded complacently.

"It wasn't a lot of work. Just ten words: I, Inspector DeKok, report that there is nothing to report."

For a moment it seemed as if the Commissaris would literally explode. Then he found his voice.

"OUT!" he roared.

DeKok left.

* * *

"Were you two at it again?"

DeKok grimaced.

"He wanted a report," was the simple answer.

Vledder shook his head.

"But why don't you try to be nice? Try to accommodate him a little?"

DeKok snorted.

"Just because he had his foot in his mouth when he talked to the Judge-Advocate, I have to make a report. It's crazy."

"But he's our boss," said Vledder mildly.

"Yes, I know that. But I can hardly be expected to tell him every hour of the day, or night, what we have been doing."

"Well," said Vledder soothingly, "you've known him longer than anybody. And he really doesn't bother us all that much, you know. He just likes to be kept informed."

"Yeah, he was that way at the Academy, too. Always sticking his nose in everybody's business," growled DeKok, refusing to be soothed.

"You were at the Academy together?" asked Vledder, his ears pricking up at this startling bit of news.

"Never mind," answered DeKok. "What about some coffee?"

"I've something better for you," laughed Vledder. "I've cousin Robert, outside on the bench."

"Cousin Robert? Robert Hoveneer?"

"Yes, he wants to talk to you."

DeKok nodded.

"All right, take him into an interrogation room, this place is too crowded."

Vledder looked a bit mystified as he rose to comply with DeKok's request. The busy, crowded detective room usually did not seem to bother DeKok at all.

"And call Leeuwarden and ask for particulars about Tjeerd Talema."

"The provincial capital?"

"Yes, we don't know what town in Friesland he's from, so we have to start somewhere."

Vledder grinned. DeKok started to think around corners again. All was well with the world.

"OK, Boss," he said, knowing full well that DeKok hated the expression.

* * *

Robert Hoveneer was pale. His fleshy, round cheeks had lost all color and had gained an unhealthy pallor.

"Do you have any trace of Mabel?"

DeKok looked at him with astonishment.

"I don't remember having received a request to find her."

The young man moved in his chair.

133

"But she has disappeared, Mr. DeKok. After the funeral she disappeared without a trace. I've looked for her everywhere. She can't be found. I'm worried. She wasn't at home either, last night."

DeKok looked searchingly at the young man. But his brains worked at full speed. Why had Robert Hoveneer shown up? Was he really worried about Mabel's welfare? The same Mabel Paddington who had so consistently refused him? The same Mabel who had accused him of murder?

"I asked Uncle Charles," continued Robert, "to inform her family in London about her disappearance, but he refused. He thought it was a bit premature."

DeKok nodded. He placed both elbows on the table and leaned forward in a conspiratorial manner. His face was so close to that of the young man, that he could hear his breathing.

"What does Mabel know?" he whispered.

Robert pulled back, as if stung. He caught his breath and his eyes peered anxiously from behind his glasses.

"Mabel," he stammered, "Mabel ... doesn't know a thing."

DeKok's eyebrows danced across his forehead.

"Isn't it strange that she persists in accusing you. That whole performance in the Chapel yesterday, was solely aimed at you."

Young Hoveneer swallowed.

"For me?" he marvelled.

DeKok nodded slowly.

"She was hoping that the terrible painting would change your mind, make you confess."

Robert laughed a hollow laugh.

"And I was supposed to turn myself in to you, just confess that I had killed Marcel?"

He laughed again, hard, hollow, without mirth. It sounded macabre and bitter.

"Something like that," admitted DeKok. "And ... in case you feel the need, I'm ready to hear your confession."

Robert's face became a mask. His face became expressionless, save for a slight tic that developed near the corner of one eye. He stared at the Inspector for a long time.

"Mabel is crazy," he exclaimed finally. "She and her idiotic paintings. She could not possibly have imagined that something like that would impress me, would bother me."

DeKok rubbed his face with both hands in a weary gesture. He leaned back in his chair.

"She's convinced that you killed Marcel. That is a serious business. That terrible death mask in the Chapel was a warning, a warning to you, to make certain that you knew she had the facts to back up her conviction."

Robert again stared at the gray Inspector. He seemed upset, confused.

"You mean to tell me that the painting in the Chapel contained some sort of information, some message for *me*?"

"Indeed."

Robert snorted suddenly.

"I don't understand anything, anymore. What information? What message? What was she trying to say?"

DeKok looked at him evenly.

"Nothing more, no less," he said, "than that *you* had killed Marcel."

Suddenly unable to remain in his seat, Hoveneer jumped up, gesticulated wildly.

"Dammit, I have ..."

He stopped, as quickly as he had started. The expression on his puffy face changed. Some color came back in his cheeks and an alert, almost cunning look came into his eyes. Slowly he sank back in his chair.

"If that painting in the Chapel," he began thoughtfully, "contained a message for me, was supposed to tell me something, there is only one logical conclusion. You're right, one way or the other, Mabel thinks she knows something that convinces her that I am the killer."

DeKok cocked his head at the young man.

"A highly interesting and original conclusion, cousin Robert," he mocked. "I asked you right from the start: What does Mabel know?"

Robert Hoveneer did not answer. Dazed he stared at the opposite wall, as if trying to gain inspiration from the mute surface. Slowly he rubbed a hand across dry lips.

DeKok leaned forward again.

"What does Mabel know?" he asked again, insistent, in a compelling tone of voice.

"How should I know?" Robert sounded irritated.

DeKok smiled thinly.

"But you saw the painting!" He paused and slowly shook his head. "No, Mabel Paddington isn't as crazy as you would have me believe, cousin Robert. Possibly she's a bit upset by the sudden demise of her fiance, but she knows full well what she's about. Therefore, if that performance in the Chapel was to make any sense at all, at all, the message on the painting would have to be very clear to the murderer."

There was a long silence. Finally Robert seemed to find his voice back.

"You forget one tiny, little detail," he said hoarsely, "I am *not* the murderer."

* * *

DeKok remained alone in the interrogation room after Robert Hoveneer had left. While the everyday crimes were routinely handled in the large detective room next door, DeKok searched frantically for a path through the labyrinth of possibilities. He could not remember ever having been involved in such a strange case. It was a mysterious murder, more mysterious than any other. There was no line, no trace, no logical thread. Everything was just a little too vague, too confusing, too silly. It irritated him no end. It was ridiculous that the victim had not yet been identified, that he did not have a clue about his background. In almost every murder case it was assumed as gospel: "Know the victim and you'll find the killer." And that was the crux of the matter. He didn't *know* the victim. Perhaps the motive for the killing was in the victim's background. Perhaps that was why the identity was so well hidden. If he could not find out anything about the victim, he would settle for the motive. That, too, would lead him to the murderer. But in order to find the motive, he had to identify the victim. It was a vicious circle. Briefly he thought about the Worm Ouroboros, the worm that was supposed to circle the Earth, without beginning and with no end. His mind would wander that way, sometimes.

Vledder noisily entered the interrogation room.

"What *have* you done to Cousin Robert? He looked like a broken man. I passed him in the corridor, he didn't even see me."

DeKok scratched the back of his neck.

"We talked together. We spoke of things. You might call it a sort of spiritual wrestling match."

Vledder grinned.

"I bet it was a one-sided wrestling match, he was just no match for you." Vledder's admiration for his mentor knew no bounds.

DeKok shook his head, raising a hand in protest.

"You shouldn't say that. There's a sharp brain behind Robert's naive, somewhat stupid, appearance. It wouldn't do at all to underestimate him. No, not at all, at all."

"Why was he here in the first place?"

"To ask if we had found any trace of Mabel Paddington."

Vledder looked worried.

"She hasn't appeared yet?"

"Apparently not. According to Robert she didn't spend the night at home, either."

"Are we going to do anything about it?"

"What would you suggest?"

"We could send a request over the wire."

DeKok raised a finger in the air and looked at it as if he had seen it for the first time. After a while he withdrew the finger and used a little finger to rub the bridge of his nose. Vledder waited patiently.

"Let's wait a bit with that," said DeKok. His voice sounded wan, exhausted. "Check with the hotel police first, see if she's registered anywhere. Ask around the Academy. Find out if she has any particular friends among the girls. She might have spent the night with one of them."

Vledder nodded.

"You want me to interrogate the girl-friends?" He sounded eager.

DeKok smiled. Slowly he rose from his chair.

"That's not our first priority," he said, a slightly disapproving tone in his voice. "What about Friesland? Found out anything there?"

"Yes, Tjeerd Talema is from Zoetekamp. I called the city registry there, but the lady that takes care of things, wasn't there. They promised to look it up and call me back."

"Zoetekamp, you said?"

"Yes."

"Barbaric names they have up North," growled DeKok. Vledder smiled.

"She wasn't available?" was DeKok's next question, disbelief in his voice.

"Yes."

"Oh."

"In Zoetekamp that's possible, you know."

The phone rang at that moment.

Vledder lifted the receiver and listened.

DeKok looked at him intently and saw the happy face of his assistant change to morose contemplation.

"What's the matter?"

Without a word Vledder replaced the receiver.

"What *is* it?" repeated DeKok.

Vledder swallowed.

"Tjeerd Talema ... doesn't exist anymore. He died three years ago."

13

With an astonished look on his face, Vledder lowered himself into his chair.

"How can that be?" he exclaimed. "You cannot die twice, now can you?"

DeKok bit his thumbnail. His face assumed a determined, stubborn look. The eyes flashed and the friendly wrinkles of his face petrified into a hard, frightening look.

"I agree," he said sharply. "A cat may have nine lives, but not a human being. A human being lives but once."

Vledder nodded.

"You mean he can only die once," he said superfluously.

"Exactly."

"But, according to the evidence we have, Tjeerd Talema died twice."

DeKok shook his head slowly.

"If the man we fished out of the Brewers Canal is Tjeerd Talema, he died *then*. I repeat, he died a few days ago, *not* three years ago."

Vledder stood up, agitated, a deep crease in his forehead.

"All right, but who died three years ago?" he wondered. "Zoetekamp may be a hole-in-the-wall, but even there the records of deaths and births are, I believe, considered error free."

DeKok moved his legs from the desk and rose slowly. With his hands deep in the pockets of his trousers, he ambled over to the window. Slowly bouncing up and down on the balls of his feet, he stared into the distance.

"I want you to keep a close eye on cousin Robert."

Vledder stood next to him.

"*Robert* Hoveneer?"

"Yes, and keep an eye out for Mabel Paddington. She knows more than she's telling and that may be dangerous."

"For whom?"

"For her."

Vledder grinned sheepishly.

"I don't understand."

"That's not necessary. But if she hasn't surfaced by the end of the week, you pull out all the stops. Police, radio, television, Interpol, she must be found."

The young inspector looked searchingly at his mentor.

"And what about you?"

"I . . . tomorrow I'm going to Zoetekamp. There must be people there who knew Tjeerd Talema when he was still alive."

* * *

Twice the horn of the *M.S. Insula* tore apart the silence. Then she slid into the harbor of Zoetekamp, slow, stately, like a large white swan. The small harbor slumbered quietly in the sun. A few fishing boats, their rigging stripped, were moored near the old, deserted wharf.

A deck-hand tossed a bight around a mooring post with practiced ease. The post creaked as it took the strain. The captain came out of the bridge house and shouted something at a group of men and women on the shore. In their typical, sober costumes, only relieved by some solid gold brooches and buttons, they looked massive. The women yelled something back and the men laughed.

When *Insula* finally finished docking and the gangway had been lowered, DeKok was the first to leave the ship. He strolled along the quay carrying a large, rectangular parcel. The atmosphere smelled of fish and tarred nets. At the end of the quay, near the wooden shed of the Municipal Fish Auction, he sat down on a bench, next to an old fisherman. The old man did not look up but continued to devote his undivided attention to a long, old-fashioned pipe.

DeKok was used to the dour, unexcitable people who lived around the Zuyder Zee. He had been born on the island of Urk when the Zuyder Zee was still a sea in its own right. Most of it had since been drained and DeKok's island had become a large hill amid endless flat-lands filled with wheat, corn and cattle. Idly he thought about the time when his father had still made a living as a fisherman on the inland sea. Today's trip to the northern province had been along long canals, or within sight of enormous dikes. The project had been started in the thirties and by now only a third of the former Zuyder Zee was still water and was now called the Ijssel *Lake*.

DeKok waited patiently and after a while the old man pushed his astrakhan hat further back on his head, took the pipe out of his mouth and asked in a friendly voice what "sir" was doing in the village.

"Paint," lied DeKok and pointed at the rectangular parcel under his arm.

The old one nodded understandingly.

"Our old lighthouse is really beautiful," he said with pride in his voice. "Better than any along the coast. A lot of strangers paint the church as well. It's from 1517 and has never needed repair. Just maintenance."

DeKok smiled politely. If time allowed, he promised, he would exert his best painter's skill on both subjects.

At his request, the old man declared himself available to guide DeKok through the network of narrow streets toward the only hotel the town could boast. The old man was garrulous in a friendly, pleasant way.

"Where does sir come from?" he asked.

"Amsterdam."

"Oh, I've been there once. I was in a bar on the Seadike and all my money was gone in an hour. Thieves, that's what they are, sir. And you don't have to bother going to the police. They're all in it together. They're practically in partnership with the thieves, you know that?"

DeKok grinned broadly.

"Bad people, the police."

They halted in front of the hotel. The Zoetekamp Coat of Arms was mounted above the heavy entrance door. Three herrings on a field blue.

The old fisherman hesitated.

"May I offer you a drink?" asked DeKok.

The old man looked at him with a humorous gleam in his eye.

"And why did sir think that I took him all the way here to Jauwkien."

DeKok looked a question at him.

"Who is Jauwkien," he asked finally.

The fisherman pointed his thumb at the hotel.

144

"The owner. A good woman. She pours the best 'double fathead' along the coast."

"A double fathead?"

The old man nodded complacently.

"We only drink *double* fatheads," he explained.

* * *

A "double fathead" turned out to be a generous quantity of *jenever*, the Dutch national drink combining the qualities of gin, vodka and aquavit with the kick of a mule. The liquid was served in a large, tulip-shaped glass with a short, narrow stem and wide base. The old fisherman visibly enjoyed his drink while he gave DeKok's cognac a suspicious look.

"Do you like that stuff?" he asked with an unbelieving look on his face. "I didn't even know Jauwkien stocked it. It's French, ain't it?"

DeKok nodded and pushed his glass closer to the old man.

"You want to try? I haven't touched it yet."

The old man made a defensive gesture.

"No, no, I'll stick to my own medicine."

DeKok looked around while he slowly sipped from his cognac. It was not of the same quality as that served by Little Lowee, but not bad, not bad at all, he thought.

The bar of the "Zoetekamp Arms" had an unorthodox but undeniably homey atmosphere. The big canopy over the old-fashioned bar was decorated with old, black-tarred nets, green, glass floats and dried-out cork beacons. The ceiling was almost invisible because of the large collection of stuffed sea animals that seemed to descend from every square inch of the heavy, blackened oak beams that supported the floors above. In the center of the room a beautifully executed

145

model of an old fishing boat took pride of place on a highly polished lee-board from an earlier era.

It was busy in the "Zoetekamp Arms". The patrons, mostly old men, drank their "double fatheads" under loud conversation, or sipped thoughtfully while pondering one of the several checker games that were in progress.

After studying the interior for a long time, DeKok stood up and walked over to what he thought to be the best strategic position. With the large, rectangular parcel under his arm he approached an empty table against the wall. To attract some additional attention, he purposely knocked a chair over. The movement was completely natural, as if he had not seen the chair. But it had the desired result. Everybody in the bar paused and looked at him.

He slowly removed the cover from the packet and revealed the painting. He propped it up on the table, against the wall. The forceful portrait in vibrant ochers seemed to act like a magnet on the eyes of the beholders. The talking stopped, the "double fatheads" rested motionless on the surfaces where they were placed and the checker pieces were forgotten.

An old fisherman came closer to get a better look.

"But . . . that's . . . that's Talema's boy," he stammered. "It's him in . . . the flesh."

Feigning indifference, DeKok shrugged his shoulders in a nonchalant gesture.

"I don't know his name," he lied. "I happened to meet him and I asked if I could paint him. I thought he had a remarkable, expressive face."

The guests of the "Zoetekamp Arms" gathered in a half-circle around the painting. Even Jauwkien had left her customary place behind the bar.

"It's Tjeerd," she declared decisively.

146

The others nodded agreement.

"When did you paint him?"

DeKok looked at the Junoesque barkeeper.

"About four weeks ago."

A strange silence fell on the room. The men looked from the detective to the portrait and back. The looks in their eyes were suspicious, almost hostile.

"*When* did you say?" There was no denying the hint of a threat in Jauwkien's voice.

"About four weeks ago," repeated DeKok evenly.

The old fisherman shook his head vehemently.

"That's impossible," he exclaimed heatedly. "Tjeerd Talema died three years ago. I, myself, was at the funeral."

* * *

DeKok pushed his hat forward and looked up. The sign over the gate announced "LAST RESTING PLACE" in large, gilded letters. In exchange for a second "double fathead" the old fisherman had declared himself prepared to guide DeKok to the cemetery and to point out the grave of Tjeerd Talema.

The grave digger and custodian of the Zoetekamp Cemetery, a simple man with a large, round head and dull, lackluster eyes, removed the heavy chain and pushed open the wrought-iron gates. The heavy hinges shrieked in protest. The grave digger took off his cap.

"After you," he said with a broad grin on his ugly, but friendly face.

DeKok fished a tip out of one of his pockets and followed the old fisherman over the gravel paths.

"Tjeerd was related to me, you know."

DeKok glanced at the old man.

147

"Related?"

The old man nodded, as if remembering something almost forgotten.

"Yes, he was the child of my mother's niece by marriage. The whole village is more or less related to one another. Tjeerd's parents died young. He was still just a boy when he became an orphan. He was brought up by Grandma." A tender smile lit up his craggy face. "Some woman. I used to court her in my younger days."

"Is she still alive?"

"Who?"

"Grandma?"

The old man shook his head.

"No, been dead for years," he answered sadly.

He took a few more steps and kicked a gravestone with his wooden shoe.

"Here she is."

He paused for just a moment, but then continued on, keeping his face averted from DeKok.

"Tjeerd Talema had a set of brains to be proud of," he said. "He was barely fifteen when Teacher Bos said that he couldn't teach him anything else."

DeKok pushed his lower lip forward.

"My, my," he said with just the right amount of admiration in his tone.

The old man nodded.

"Well, after that he had to leave the village, you understand. He had to go to Holland." Like most people in the northern province, he was never totally reconciled to being a part of the Netherlands. There was a lot of the Scots in the Frisians, reflected DeKok. They were a part of the nation, but considered themselves different, separate. They even had their own language.

He made some meaningless sounds, encouraging the old man to continue.

"Oh, yes, he went to study Law, I think. In any case, he wasn't going to be no minister. There was a lot of hub-bub about that in the family."

"Why?"

The old man shrugged his shoulders reluctantly.

"Tradition. Anybody in the village who studies, especially when they have to go south for it, becomes either a minister, or a doctor. Tjeerd wanted something else." He paused. "Actually, he wanted something else all his life."

"What was the cause of death?"

"Something to do with his heart, I think. Leastwise, that's what I remember. Hoekstra, our young doctor explained it at the time, but I've forgotten."

* * *

The old man stopped at the end of a side path, near a beautiful, white marble stone. He lifted his cap with a devout gesture. His gray hair blew in the breeze.

"Here he rests," he said softly.

DeKok followed the old man's example. With his hat in his hand he stood next to the fisherman and looked at the stone.

Here rests
TJEERD TALEMA
*

27 December, 19..
12 February, 19..
*

He, who has conquered
even death . . .

"You see," said the old man, "there is no way you could have painted him four weeks ago."

DeKok did not answer. He stared at the stone as if fixated by the slab of marble. Again and again he read the text. He could not shake the feeling that the solution of the mystery was within his grasp, but the necessary connecting spark would not come.

"Who was responsible for placing the stone?"

"Dirk Hoekstra."

"The young doctor?"

"Yes. He and Tjeerd were friends. Dirk organized the funeral too."

"What about the text?"

"The doctor selected that himself."

"A nice text."

The old man nodded agreement.

"The family was very happy with it."

DeKok looked at the old man from the corner of his eyes.

"Happy?"

"Yes, pleased, happy, whatever. We had not expected it."

"How's that?"

The old man gave DeKok a sad look.

"Dr. Hoekstra, you see, doesn't believe. Not like us. He's an atheist."

14

Suddenly the old fisherman stopped in the middle of the narrow street. His legs spread, his pipe clamped into a corner of his mouth, he looked as if he stood at the helm of his old fishing boat, facing the elements. A hard, expressionless face stared at DeKok. He looked as if he would never move again.

"Why do you want to see the young doctor?" the voice was irritated, almost angry.

DeKok tapped his own chest.

"My heart bothers me," he lied.

The old man snorted, releasing a large cloud of smoke from his pipe.

"There's nothing wrong with your heart. You're making that up. It's not nice to mock your health, you know." He cocked his head at the gray sleuth. "You want to know something?" he asked.

"Well?"

"You're no painter. Nossir, you're not."

DeKok managed to express amazement.

"Really?"

The old man shook his head. The stubbornness for which the Frisians were well known in a country full of stubborn people was evident on the old man's face.

"No. We just passed our old church, the most picturesque spot in our entire village . . . you didn't even look at it."

DeKok leaned toward him.

"Shall I tell you something?"

"I'm listening," said the old man implacably.

"You're right . . . I am no painter."

The fisherman gave him a suspicious look.

"I know that. But what *are* you?"

DeKok did not answer at once. He wondered how far he could trust the old man, how much he could take him into his confidence.

"I'm an inspector," he said softly.

"Police?"

DeKok nodded.

"And I'll buy you another 'double fathead' if you keep it to yourself for the time being."

The old man's face lit up. The stubborn, suspicious look was replaced by a friendly smile.

"I'll be silent like the grave," he declared.

DeKok pulled his lower lip and let it plop back, one of his most annoying habits. He did it several times. A pensive look came into his eyes.

"Sometimes . . . sometimes," he said slowly, "not even the grave is silent."

* * *

Dr. D. Hoekstra, Physician, was engraved with elegant letters on a shiny brass plate next to the door. On the other side of the door was a white painted sign which stated the consulting hours in bold, black block letters.

DeKok looked at his watch and verified that the consulting hour for that day was just about over.

The old fisherman made a vague gesture.

"If you need me again . . . you can find me at the harbor. Same spot, on the bench." He walked away, but returned after a few paces. "Don't let him give you nothing," he said with a nod toward the door.

"Give?" marveled DeKok. "Why not?"

"Last month he gave one my friends some of those little red pills . . . a week later we had to bury him." He shook his head. "I just don't trust young doctors. You see, they experiment too often. If you ask me . . . eh," he hesitated, then finished in a rush: "If you ask me Tjeerd Talema didn't have to die, either."

"What?"

The old man rubbed his stubbly chin with a thoughtful look in his eyes.

"Well, yes. Look, you don't have to believe the rumors that are flying around. But it *is* a fact, you know, that Tjeerd looked remarkably healthy, just days before he died."

* * *

The walls were covered with the usual announcements from the Red Cross, urging the donation of blood and from the National Health Organization, warning about the dangers of TB. It was a sign of the times that even in this remote village a poster prominently promoted "safe sex" and warned about the dangers of AIDS.

A number of Zoetekamp's women were seated on hard, straight-backed chairs, disdaining the comfortable, modern furniture. They looked strangely at the detective. DeKok greeted them shyly and as if to prove that he was one of them, placed himself on the last remaining uncomfortable chair in the waiting room. He placed his decrepit little hat on his knees as if it was the most fashionable top hat and waited patiently until, one by one, the women had been called in by the sharp little buzzer over the door to the consulting room. It did not take long. The young doctor seemed to make rapid diagnostic decisions.

When it was his turn to be summoned by the buzzer, he delayed purposefully. Only after the buzzer had sounded for the second time, a bit longer, did he get up to enter the consulting room.

* * *

Dr. Hoekstra was a tall, lean man with thick, dark-blond hair, prominent, high cheeks bones and a pair of bright green, penetrating eyes. He wore a stark white surgical coat with short sleeves. His arms were tanned and well muscled. He emerged from behind his desk and stretched out a strong, cool hand toward the detective. Their eyes crossed momentarily, but the greeting was strictly formal, professional. Immediately after a short handshake, the doctor resumed his seat behind the desk and took out a card from a desk drawer.

"Name?"

"DeKok ... with kay-oh-kay."

"Profession?"

DeKok hesitated. He did not want to play all his cards at once.

"Insurance broker," he lied. It was the first profession that came to mind.

The doctor looked up.

"Are you planning to settle in the village?"

154

DeKok smiled.

"Is there any business here?" he asked, dodging the question. "I specialize in life insurance."

A vague look came into the doctor's eyes.

"Life insurance?"

DeKok nodded.

"It is a good living," he sighed. "But I think that the Law should prohibit life insurance. It's such a scurrilous agreement."

The young doctor replaced his pen on the desk. Apparently the remark had touched something.

"Scurrilous? But why?"

"The name is all wrong. Life is not insured, but death."

The doctor stared at him as if he came from another planet.

"I think," he said thoughtfully, "That a lot of people would disagree with you. Life insurance doesn't have to be scurrilous. It's not necessarily obscene, or improper. For many people it's a calming, reassuring feeling to know that their near and dear will remain provided for after their death."

DeKok forced an expression of sheer admiration on his face.

"The next time I have a reluctant client, I'll send him to you. Very good. You'd be able to sell *me* a life insurance policy."

The doctor laughed. A cheerful, open laugh.

"Shoemaker, stick to your last," he grinned. "I better stick to my pills and potions." The friendly, lively face changed back to a professional mask. "What are your complaints?" The tone of voice, too, had changed back to a professional level.

Despite the seriousness of the visit, the young doctor had endeared himself to DeKok. The old-fashioned saying about the shoemaker, reminded DeKok of his old mother. A very wise woman who seemed to have an inexhaustible store of sayings, Bible texts and quotations for every possible occasion.

DeKok pointed at his chest.

"It's my heart."

"What's the matter with it?"

DeKok smiled shyly.

"I . . . sometimes I've the feeling," he said gravely, "that its beat is much too volatile, too spirited for my age."

The doctor reached across the desk and took his pulse.

"How old are you?"

DeKok did not answer.

The doctor looked up at him.

"How old are you?" he repeated impatiently.

DeKok pressed his lips together. Then he answered slowly.

"Just like Tjeerd Talema," he said grimly, "too young to die."

With a sudden, violent movement the young doctor leaned back in his chair. His face was suddenly red and his bright, green eyes flashed malevolently. He stretched out an arm to his visitor.

"I demand that you immediately leave my consulting room."

Slowly, sadly, DeKok shook his head.

"I'll have to disappoint you," he said with a hint of irony in his voice. "There's no way that I can give in to your friendly request until you have explained in detail, and to my complete satisfaction, how your friend Tjeerd came to die."

Angrily the doctor leaned closer to the gray sleuth.

"That is none of your damned business," he roared.

DeKok shrugged his shoulders in a manner certain to irritate.

"I could easily dig up the official death certificate from the register. The death certificate *you* signed three years ago." He paused and watched the doctor slowly regain his composure. Then he continued: "I can also persuade the Judge-Advocate to issue an order for exhumation. I can probably get that on just the evidence of the gossip in town."

Dr. Hoekstra fell back in his chair. The color had completely drained from his face. Nervous tics were visible around the eyes and the mouth and he blinked several times.

"Who *are* you?" he asked hoarsely.

DeKok produced his most winning smile.

"I came here under false colors," he admitted calmly. "I'm no insurance broker. I'm a cop."

"Oh!?"

"Yes. I came to Zoetekamp this morning, from Amsterdam, because I'm interested in the way Tjeerd Talema died."

The doctor nodded slowly.

"I know there's a lot of gossip in the village. Please forget my earlier outburst. It's extremely difficult to defend oneself against gossip, against rumors, innuendos." He smoothed his hair with a tired gesture. "Tjeerd Talema was my friend . . . the only friend I ever had. Do you really believe that I would *not* use all my knowledge and expertise to save him?"

DeKok looked at the younger man for several minutes. He searched the face for signs of insincerity. He did not believe the doctor, but could not discover the lie. There was more to it all than appeared on the surface.

"What was the cause of death?"

"For years Tjeerd had lived a wild life, unrestrained drinking, little sleep, wild parties. Sometimes it marks a person. Sometimes it's fatal. Tjeerd died of 'Manager's Disease', an unscientific term for stress. It has only been recently recognized as a severe disorder."

"Stress?"

"Yes. Actually a coronary. The heart simply gave out as a result of excessive physical and mental activity over an extended period of time. I stated as much on the Death Certificate."

DeKok nodded.

"So, he died a natural death?"

"Yes, not very remarkable. It was merely unusual that Tjeerd was still relatively so very young."

DeKok rubbed his face.

"Then how do you explain the gossip in the village?"

"Well, you know how it is in a village. Everybody knows everything about everybody . . . except the person in question. That person is in the dark."

"You have no suspicions?"

The doctor made a vague gesture, as if trying to dismiss the question. Then, somewhat reluctantly he answered.

"I think the carpenter started it all."

DeKok looked incredulous.

"The carpenter?"

Dr. Hoekstra smiled wanly.

"Yes. We have a lot of old-fashioned customs here. One of those involves the carpenter. It's customary to alert the carpenter in case of death. He comes and measures the corpse and starts making the coffin that day. Every coffin is custom-built, so to speak." He took a deep breath, sighed. "It so happens that our carpenter is a rather strange person, a drunk, who celebrates every death with joy and happiness."

"What?"

"Oh, yes. First he has a few drinks when he comes to measure the corpse. Have you heard about our local drink, the 'double fathead'?"

DeKok merely nodded, willing him to continue.

"I measured it once," continued the doctor, "a 'double fathead' contains about as much alcohol as any three normal sized drinks combined. Anyway, the carpenter always has a few when he measures the corpse. As far as I know he drinks steadily while he works and then he has as many as he can hold when he delivers the finished coffin. It's not unusual to see him stagger from the house of the bereaved long before the first visitors arrive for the wake. He seldom makes it to the funeral."

DeKok could not help but laugh.

"You're putting me on," he laughed.

The doctor shook his head.

"I swear to you," he said earnestly. "It's true. And nobody dares refuse him, let alone get a carpenter from the next village. They're all afraid of the old knacker."

"Knacker?" DeKok was not sure he had heard right.

"Yes, that's what they call him. He's a sinister figure. He prefers to work on his coffins at night. He sings loudly when he's not drinking and bangs away. Every coffin is completely hand-made, you know. He uses no power tools. It's an eerie sound when you walk by his shop at night."

"And the gossip?"

The doctor grinned sadly.

"It's obvious. Tjeerd died in this house. I wanted to prevent the usual *bacchanalia* and didn't offer him a drop.

After he delivered the coffin, I paid him and again refused to offer him a drink. I just sent him on his way."

"Sober?"

"Sober," repeated the doctor tonelessly. "At least as sober as he usually is. Ever since that day the wildest rumors about me have been circulated and I lost a number of patients to the old doctor in the next village. It's only about seven miles from here, you see. I have been advised to sell, or give up, the practice. But I'm from around here. I can be just as stubborn as the rest of the Frisians. Nobody is going to chase me away . . . especially not a knacker." He said the last word with a considerable amount of disgust in his voice.

Both remained silent for a long time. DeKok thought over the interview in detail. It was one of his gifts. At such moments his brain worked like a tape-recorder. He could recall every word, every intonation, each gesture. He looked up. The man across the desk was likeable. But he doubted whether the young doctor had been completely straightforward. On the contrary.

Slowly he took his notebook out of a pocket and slowly he flipped the pages. Then he read out loud, without warning:

Amice, I've reached the end of my odyssey. I have found her and you know what that means. It's strange, but I'm neither happy, nor bitter. My heart is empty. There are even moments that I doubt myself, feel unable to proceed with my plan. Sometimes it all seems so senseless. But whatever happens . . .

He smiled shyly.

"That's all there was," he explained apologetically. "The letter was never finished."

He replaced the notebook in his pocket, placed his almost forgotten hat on his head and without another word he walked toward the door. At the door he stopped, looked around for just a moment.

Dr. Hoekstra looked as if he had fainted. His face was as white as a sheet.

15

Leisurely DeKok strolled back to the harbor. He hoped he had treated the doctor correctly. He smiled at the simile. Reading the note had been a sudden inspiration, an impulse. It was hard to predict what the result would be. It was no more than a shot in the dark. He had the distinct feeling that he could afford few "misses" in this particular case, but this time it would do no harm. Black Sylvia's "Jacques" had written the letter, or had started to write the letter, shortly before his death. The text clearly indicated that the intended addressee knew all about the pre-history. He wrote: "I have found her . . ." There was no further indication. The friend to whom the letter was addressed knew who was being discussed. "Amice", the Latin word for friend. It might be the way one educated person would address another. Tjeerd had, apparently, studied Law. Both doctors and lawyers were familiar with more than a smattering of Latin. Why should not the young doctor be the friend? It seemed logical. The "friend" was aware of the plan, whatever that was . . . a plan about which "Jacques" had doubts. A plan he thought to be "senseless". DeKok sighed.

He searched through his pockets and found some hard candy in one of them and a few sticks of gum in another. He decided on the gum. Slowly chewing, he meditated about what he had learned so far.

Sylvia's "Jacques", turned out to be Mabel's "Marcel" who stayed in *The Blue Pitcher* and had told "Uncle Louis" in a confidential mood that his real name was Tjeerd Talema. The same Tjeerd Talema, or so it was supposed, had been fished from the waters of the Brewers Canal with a smashed skull as recently as the 15th of March. So far so good, thought DeKok, except for the fact that he had, as yet, been unable to track down the killer.

But now, thought DeKok, as Vledder is fond of saying, it doesn't compute. Because according to the Zoetekamp town registry, the same Tjeerd died more than three years ago. A young doctor declared that the victim had died of a coronary and a gravestone was mute witness to the inevitable result.

DeKok grinned sadly to himself. Perhaps the best thing to do, he mused, was to take the next boat back to Amsterdam and ask the Commissaris in all humility if someone else could take over the case. The puzzle of a Tjeerd Talema who died twice bothered him. Nobody dies twice. No matter what the records in Zoetekamp showed ... it was impossible. Tjeerd died on the 14th of March and not three years ago.

He leaned forward in order to duck beneath the clotheslines that had been stretched across the center of the road. Who, he asked himself, is buried in Zoetekamp. Or are there possibly *two* Tjeerds? Annoyed with himself he shook his head. That was most unlikely. Even if they had been twins, they would have had different first names and nobody had said anything about twins. Perhaps twins that had been separated immediately after birth?

He snorted in disgust. It was possible, but too pat, too convenient. He had never heard of such a case, other than in fiction. But it *was* possible, he admonished himself. It would not do to neglect any possibilities.

Without remembering where he had walked, he discovered that he had reached the harbor. The old fisherman, as promised, was seated on the bench next to the Fish Auction. When the old man saw DeKok approach, he carefully tapped his pipe against a wooden shoe.

"Did he give you something?" he asked curiously.

DeKok shook his head.

"No, we talked a bit about Tjeerd."

"And?"

"He died of a coronary."

The old man nodded thoughtfully.

"Now I remember," he said. "That's what the doctor called it, a coronary." Carefully he put the clay pipe into an inside pocket. "I'm not surprised that young people die of heart failure. I can't remember how many times I died of heart disease, in my younger days? Man ... at least three times a week."

DeKok's eyebrows rippled briefly. For just a moment the old man seemed transfixed. Then he obviously decided that his old eyes had deceived him. With a last, furtive glance at DeKok's forehead, he listened to the question.

"You mean to tell me that Tjeerd didn't die of a coronary?"

The old man shook his head.

"Maybe Tjeerd suffered from a *broken* heart ... but certainly not from a *failing* heart." He stood up. "You want to know something, Inspector, as long as I can remember, and that's a few years, nobody in *our* family ever died because of a bad ticker." He thumbed himself heavily on the chest. "And I mean this ticker, here."

"So, what *did* he die of?"

"Yes, well . . . you should have asked *that* of the young doctor."

DeKok pressed his lips together to prevent an angry outburst. He had the sinking feeling that he was drifting further and further away from the solution.

"Who's the *knacker*?"

The old man smiled.

"Did the doctor talk about him?"

DeKok nodded.

"He accuses the knacker of the gossip that's being spread about him."

The old man looked annoyed.

"The knacker is a good man. I know him. His only vice is that he likes a 'double fathead' now and again. Who can blame him for that?"

"Nobody."

"Right! That's the way it is. The young doctor just made a mistake, is all. He thought that knacker would forget everything after just one bottle of jenever." He grinned to himself and scratched the back of his neck. "No, for *that* he'd have to drink at least a *barrel*."

DeKok looked up at the old man in surprise.

"You're telling me," he said with disbelief in his voice, "that the doctor gave him a bottle?"

The old man nodded with conviction.

"Yes, a whole bottle. He could have had as many as he liked."

Somberly DeKok stared at the tiny harbor. He was at a loss. The doctor had been quite positive about having refused the carpenter any booze.

"Where can I find the knacker?"

The old man waved into the direction of the village.

"In his shed. Griet of Lange Meindert died yesterday. He's probably working on the coffin now."

DeKok absorbed the information. How typical of this part of Holland, he thought. A person by the name of Meindert and the nickname "tall" had a daughter. The daughter had died. But she was still referred to as her father's daughter. No mention of the Mother, a husband, if any, or even a family name. Some habits died hard, he thought. Could that have caused an error in the records?

Misunderstanding DeKok's silence, the old man offered:

"I don't mind showing you the way. It's rather hard to find."

"Please," answered DeKok.

With a delightfully transparent gesture, the wily old man rubbed the back of his neck.

"It's just that I feel so dry, just now. Also ... if I remember correctly, you still owe me a 'double fathead'."

DeKok laughed.

"You're absolutely right. The knacker can wait. We both need a pick-me-up."

They walked toward the "Zoetekamp Arms" with a common goal in mind.

* * *

As soon as they entered the taproom, Jauwkien approached them with a happy smile on her face and a beaming expression. She felt around in one of the pockets of her voluminous apron and produced five notes of a hundred guilders each. Slowly and with pride, she counted them out into DeKok's hand.

"This is for you," she said.

DeKok looked at her with astonishment.

"For me?"

She nodded.

"I sold your painting."

"What!?"

She laughed at him, as a mother would laugh at a precocious child.

"Good price, don't you think?"

DeKok swallowed.

"But . . . but," he stammered, "I . . . I didn't want to sell the painting at all."

The innkeeper's face fell.

"Surely you don't make paintings to keep them yourself?"

DeKok clapped his hands to his face. It had been stupid to leave the painting in the taproom.

"Who bought it?" he groaned.

"Ilona."

"What Ilona?"

"Ilona Kastanje. She's always been crazy about Tjeerd. She came in about half an hour ago, all in a dither. Somebody had told her that you had made Tjeerd's portrait. News travels fast," she concluded complacently.

DeKok stared at her, willing her to continue. Within seconds Jauwkien obliged.

"She sat on the chair, over there," continued Jauwkien. "She stared at the painting for a while. You could see it touched her, affected her. Then she said she wanted to buy it and asked how much it was." The innkeeper displayed a comical grin on her fine features. "I told her five hundred.

I thought, who is going to pay that kind of money for a painting. It doesn't even have a frame."

"What happened?"

"She left without a word and five minutes later she was back and put the money on the counter. She took the painting."

DeKok nodded. For a moment he seemed nonplussed. Then he picked up the bank notes and pulled the old fisherman toward the door.

"Come, my friend, show me the house of Ilona Kastanje."

The old man protested vehemently.

"What about my 'double fathead'?" he whined.

DeKok grinned.

"Later . . . later, I'll buy you a whole bottle."

* * *

From a distance the old man pointed at an elegant villa surrounded by a well-maintained garden.

"That's where she lives."

DeKok made a gesture as if counting money, rubbing his thumb against his crooked index finger.

"That place looks like money."

The old man grinned gleefully.

"Yes, they ain't exactly forced to watch the pennies."

"Does Ilona live alone?"

"With her mother."

"Not married?"

"No."

"Not good looking enough?"

The old man pushed his lower lip forward, as if weighing his answer.

"Ilona is a very good looking child." There was genuine admiration in his voice. "You know what I mean, not too much meat on her bones, but padded in all the right places. She's had suitors by the score. But . . . what can you do, she had set her heart on Tjeerd. When he died, she hove to, so to speak. Oh, in the beginning people had real understanding for her sorrow. Of course, they did. Everybody knew she'd been crazy about Tjeerd. But after a while they started to blame her, considered she was overdoing it, the grief, I mean." The old man snorted his own indignation. "Really, considering everything she's got to offer a man, it's almost a sin."

"What do you mean?"

The old man made an impatient gesture.

"She rejected all offers. Just like that. Mind, not from just anybody, either. There are whispers that she even refused the young doctor."

"Hoekstra?"

The old man worried the gold ring in his ear.

"Yes. Shortly after Tjeerd's death he used to visit her regularly. You understand . . . people will talk."

DeKok rubbed the bridge of his nose with a little finger.

"I see, and the community decided that the doctor may have given Mother Nature a helping hand."

The old man shrugged his shoulders, glanced at DeKok with a guileless face.

"It would be easy to do, for a doctor."

DeKok nodded thoughtfully.

"Yes," he agreed, "for a doctor it would be easy."

16

Holding on to the doorknob, Ilona Kastanje looked searchingly at the Inspector. The look in her eyes was cool, arrogant, almost hostile.

"What do you want?"

DeKok smiled winningly.

"I came to get my painting."

She blinked her eyes and bit her lower lip. Her hand tightened around the doorknob, ready to slam the door in DeKok's face.

"*Your* painting?"

DeKok nodded brightly.

"I left it in the taproom of the 'Zoetekamp Arms' because I had some errands and didn't want to carry it around. The innkeeper sold it without my knowing about it, without my permission."

Her expression became even, unreadable.

"You want more money?"

DeKok shook his head.

"No, no," he assured her hastily, a pained expression on his face. "The painting isn't for sale."

"Oh!?"

"I would like to explain."

She hesitated. Then she opened the door wide.

"Come in."

DeKok stepped past her. The foyer of the villa was roomy with a high ceiling. The gray sleuth hung his coat and hat on a beautifully carved, antique coat rack. He looked around. An enormous Frisian grandfather clock with shiny brass weights told him that he had been running around Zoetekamp for more than four hours. And how far had he progressed? He raked his fingers through his hair and grinned at his reflection in a mirror. The veil that hung around the mystery of the victim seemed to get more and more clouded.

The young woman led him to a cozy sitting room dominated by an immense, oak fireplace and restrained, ornamental paintings on the walls. She gestured invitingly to a long, wide bench with lots of cushions.

"Please sit down."

She seated herself across from him in an easy chair, neatly, the slender legs tightly pressed together and the hem of her skirt pulled down below the knees.

"You're an artiste?" She pronounced the word in the French manner and seemed to be able to convey both contempt and admiration in the same sentence.

DeKok did not answer. His gaze travelled shamelessly from her slim ankles upward and finally came to rest on her dark, almond shaped eyes that contrasted in a strange, exciting way with the long, blonde hair. The old fisherman had been right, Ilona Kastanje had a lot to offer a man.

"You're a painter?" Her voice was fuller, less sharp, the undertone of contempt had disappeared.

DeKok smiled.

"No, I'm no painter."

"Dealer?" The sharpness hovered again on the edges.

DeKok shook his head. He took the five hundred guilders from his pocket and gave it to her.

"I'm sorry, but I have to nullify the sale."

She accepted the money carelessly and stood up. DeKok followed her with his eyes when she left the room. She came back a few minutes later and leaned the painting against the bench. Her eyes were red. She had obviously been crying.

"Did ... you ... did you know Tjeerd Talema?" she asked, controlling a sob with some effort.

DeKok swallowed.

"No," he hesitated. "I never knew him. That's to say, not in the way you mean. But I have been very busy, the last few days, trying to get to know him better."

Confused, she looked at her visitor.

"What ... what do you mean?"

DeKok scratched the back of his neck. He was at a loss about the best approach. According to village gossip she loved Tjeerd dearly. But was that true? Was it her only role? What was her relation with the young doctor?

"Tjeerd's death," he said, still in doubt, "must have been a shock to you."

She nodded slowly, without conviction.

"It was quite a shock."

"Do you ever visit the cemetery?"

"No."

"There's a beautiful stone on the grave."

"I know."

"The text especially touched me."

She looked at him, suspiciously, searchingly.

"He, who has conquered even death ..."

DeKok nodded.

"That's what it says. It took me a long time before I discovered the deeper meaning. Now I understand what was meant: some dead don't die . . . They live on in our memory." He picked up the painting. "Is that what he looked like?" he asked.

She did not answer at once. Her lower lip trembled.

"He . . . I . . . I don't remember him that old."

"But it *is* Tjeerd?"

"Yes."

DeKok pointed at the painting.

"As far as I can tell, he was an extremely fascinating man. In the village they whisper that you loved him. Why didn't you marry him, at the time?"

She moved uneasily in her chair. Her dark eyes glittered.

"What business is it of yours?" she exclaimed angrily.

DeKok rubbed the bridge of his nose with a little finger. Then he looked at it as if he had seen it for the first time. He withdrew the little finger and replaced it with an index finger. He used it to point at the painting.

"I," he declared, "am interested in his death."

"His death?"

DeKok nodded slowly, making a vague gesture with the hand that had just pointed at the portrait.

"I wonder *how* exactly Tjeerd died, three years ago. I presume you were at his bedside?"

Slowly she rose. The light from the window threw a halo around her hair. She walked over to the mantelpiece and moved an ornament a fraction of an inch. Then she turned around and looked down on him. She looked regal, imposing, yet oddly vulnerable.

"You're from the police."

DeKok smiled ruefully.

"Exactly right. I'm with the Amsterdam Municipal Police. Homicide."

"I suspected you might be police when you first came in. You're dressed all wrong for somebody involved in art. Too . . . too conforming." She walked back to her chair and sat down again.

"Tjeerd's painting was the bait?"

DeKok pursed his lips.

"More or less. Actually, I just wanted to be sure that we were both speaking of the same person."

She looked at him in surprise. A deep crease marred her forehead, just above the nose. On her, decided DeKok, it looked attractive.

"Are you really interested in Tjeerd's death?"

"Yes, I am."

"But why?"

"Because . . . eh . . . because he died *twice*."

"*Twice*?"

DeKok nodded, watching her reaction.

"Once in Zoetekamp," he said, "and once again in Amsterdam."

She looked at him with wide, frightened eyes.

"But that's impossible. Really, that's impossible. I was at the funeral. Tjeerd is here . . . in the cemetery. You've seen the stone yourself." She spoke rapidly, stumbling over the words. "The one in Amsterdam wasn't Tjeerd. I mean, it couldn't have been Tjeerd. It had to be somebody else."

Slowly, regretfully, DeKok shook his head.

"You were at his deathbed?"

"No."

"You weren't warned?"

She adjusted her skirt, pulled it down an invisible millimeter.

175

"I knew that Tjeerd had come back to the village. You know how fast news travels. I knew he was staying with Douwe . . . that is, Dirk Hoekstra. I didn't know he was sick. I waited for him to come visit me. I don't mind telling you I waited with some excitement for his visit. But he didn't go anywhere. He didn't show himself. Anywhere."

DeKok absorbed this. With one part of his mind he noted how the common name "Dirk" was bastardized to "Douwe" in the barbaric language of the northern provinces. Then he admonished himself. His long stay in Amsterdam made him sometimes forget that he had grown up in close kinship to these same people. In the distant past, when his father's fishing boat probably docked in Zoetekamp to allow the crew to attend church services on Sunday. In those days not a single fisherman would remain at sea on Sunday. They made for the nearest port on Saturday night, regardless of the weather, or the catch. These people might appear barbaric and bucolic to the sophisticated, jaded populations of the big cities, but they were also very pious, god-fearing, hard-working people. The salt of the earth, really. All this flashed through his mind. It made his task both easier and harder at the same time.

"What happened next?" he asked.

"Then I suddenly heard that Tjeerd had died."

"Who told you?"

"I don't remember. I think my mother told me."

"Did you go see him then?"

She shook her head.

"Douwe wouldn't allow it. I had gone through a rough time, not long before it happened. I was very sick. It took months to recover."

"Doctor Hoekstra feared a relapse?"

"Yes."

DeKok looked at her sharply.

"Your illness, did it have anything to do with Tjeerd?"

She nodded imperceptibly.

"In retrospect," she sighed, "I wonder if I didn't overdo it, pretended too much. Time heals all wounds. Recently, very recently, I was able to take a step back, review things more objectively. But then ... then, I couldn't handle it. To me it was as if the world had come to an end. Tjeerd and I, we were friends since kindergarten, since before kindergarten, actually. It was always that way, all the way through High School. Right up to the time that Tjeerd went to Holland." She paused. DeKok suppressed a smile at the mention of "Holland" as a foreign country. After a long pause she continued.

"We belonged together," she whispered. "We belonged together. Forever. Everybody said so ... and it was so."

Again she paused. She raised her head and looked DeKok full in the face. She smiled, not sad, but with acceptance.

"It's been years since I have bared my soul like this. And now ... especially in front of a stranger." But she did not sound embarrassed.

DeKok grinned conspiratorially. A grinning DeKok was irresistible. She looked at him, mesmerized.

"I could have made a career as a father-confessor," said DeKok with a twinkle in his eyes. She responded spontaneously with a bright smile.

Then DeKok became serious again. His face became expressionless, businesslike.

"I take it that Tjeerd ruined the rosy prospects for the future?"

She sighed deeply.

"You could say that. One day I received a letter from him. From Utrecht. He told me that he loved someone else. Just like that. According to his letter he had only recently experienced true love. Our relationship, he wrote, compared to that, was little more than a roll-in-the-hay among friends."

DeKok pushed his lower lip forward.

"Charming," he commented, "is that really how he put it?"

"Yes."

"Less than elegant."

"Indeed. It was anything but elegant. Men can never find the right tone in that sort of situation. He *did* ask for understanding and I wrote back that I was full of understanding and I wished him and his 'love' all possible happiness." She sat back in her chair. The long, slender fingers showed white at the knuckles as she gripped the armrests in an effort to control herself.

"I . . . I never saw him after that," she added.

Both remained silent for a long time.

After a while Inspector DeKok lifted the painting on his knees and turned it toward her.

"What do you think of it?"

"Very good. Beautiful."

DeKok nodded agreement.

"A little while ago you made a peculiar remark. You said, and I quote: *I don't remember him that old.*"

Nervously she curled a strand of her glorious hair around her fingers.

"Yes, you see, the eyes . . . Tjeerd . . . . Tjeerd." She swallowed, wrestling with her tears. "I don't remember him that old," she concluded lamely.

DeKok replaced the painting on the floor.

"What happened to his *love*?"

"He married her."

DeKok looked up with expectation on his face.

"Married?"

"Yes, about eighteen months before his death."

"Where?"

"I think in Utrecht. Tjeerd was a junior partner in a law firm there."

"What was her name?"

"I don't know." She shrugged her shoulders. "I never knew her name."

DeKok looked thoughtfully at nothing in particular.

"So, she didn't come to Zoetekamp with him?"

Ilona Kastanje smiled a bitter smile.

"No ... Tjeerd Talema was alone ... he died alone." Her every word dripped with bitterness and hate. "His ... his *love*," the word was spoken with all the venom possible, "his so-called *love* wasn't even at the funeral."

17

With the painting under his arm, DeKok ambled through the friendly little town. It was amazing, he thought, how quickly he had been able to acclimatize himself to the atmosphere of his early days. Most people greeted him politely as he passed, something that just wasn't done in the big cities. He grinned softly to himself. The fast and efficient gossip mill must have identified him to most of the population by now.

He realized that he was starting to recognize the narrow streets. The harbor had long since ceased to be a problem. He could find it blindfolded. From there he would pass the bakeshop and a miniature supermarket, a few other landmarks and arrive at Jauwkien's. Even the names started to become familiar to him. He hoped the old fisherman would still be waiting behind his "double fathead". He would still need him as a guide, despite his growing familiarity with the town. The "knacker", the alleged source of the town gossip, could prove to be a key figure in the mystery. But first he had to eat. His stomach growled in protest. He had eaten nothing since he left Amsterdam.

He looked at his watch. Quarter past five already. Of course, the town hall would be closed by now. No need to waste time there today. Stupid, really, not to have asked

Vledder to look up any family relations. He might have known sooner that Tjeerd Talema had been married. What happened to the wife? There was something unreal, something improbable about the whole story, he mused. Had the "great love" been cooled to the extent that the widow would not even attend the funeral? After just eighteen months? Did she not know that her husband had died? Had Dr. Hoekstra neglected to inform her?

* * *

The taproom of the "Zoetekamp Arms" was almost completely deserted. The old fisherman seemed lost at a table in the corner. He made a moody gesture toward a "double fathead" on the table in front of him.

"She kept you, I see. I've taken the liberty to have one at your expense."

DeKok placed a friendly hand on the old man's shoulder.

"Excellent, really excellent, my friend. As long as I'm in Zoetekamp you drink every single 'double fathead' at my expense."

The old man beamed.

"You might be sorry. How long are you staying?"

DeKok laughed heartily.

"It depends on the investigation. By the way, was Tjeerd married?"

The old man shook his head.

"Not as far as I know. Never heard anything like that, neither. Leastways, he never showed up here with a wife." He looked up at DeKok. "Did Ilona say he was married?"

"Yes."

"Funny. It's news to me. Must have been a missy from the big city in Holland."

DeKok nodded agreement.

"I think so. He worked in Utrecht at the time. Did anybody ever inquire about Tjeerd, after his death, I mean?"

"Who would want to know about a dead person?"

"Me."

The old man grinned a toothless smile.

"Yes, well, but you're a cop."

DeKok scratched behind his ear. There was no argument there, he thought. He sank a little further down into the chair and stretched his tired legs underneath the table.

"You know," he yawned, "I'm starving. Would you recommend eating here?"

The old man leaned toward DeKok.

"Jauwkien has fresh tongue today," he whispered. "Steamed in the best butter." He licked his lips. "That . . . and one of those pale wines . . . Believe you me, you can't get anything better nowhere else."

DeKok smiled.

"Very good, please ask her to serve for two."

The old man looked around.

"For two?"

"Yes," answered DeKok brusquely. "I take it you'll join me?"

The old man rubbed his hands with a satisfied expression.

"Of course I will. What did you think? I'll be happy to show a citified policeman how a fisherman can eat."

* * *

183

The old fisherman walked next to DeKok. His wooden shoes clattered on the cobblestones and echoed against the houses of the narrow streets. His face was red with the afterglow of the tongue and the white wine.

"You have a lot of jobs like this?"

"In Zoetekamp?"

"Yes."

"Well, whenever somebody dies an unnatural death . . ."

The old man glanced at him.

"Shall I tell you how Frerik of Red Simon died?"

DeKok grinned.

"No, thanks, one corpse is enough for the time being."

The old man shrugged his shoulders.

"I just meant to say that . . . I can find a lot of jobs for you here in the village."

They halted in front of a weathered barn at the end of an alley. A line of light was visible between the bottom of the two large doors and the dirt that seemed to form the floor of the barn. A psalm could be heard coming from the interior.

The old man raised a finger in the air.

"The knacker," he explained, "can only work when he sings."

"He's got a good voice."

"In his early days he used to sing solo in the church choir. He was also the precentor. Now we have an organ."

He kicked a wooden shoe against the barn door. The singing stopped abruptly. There was the sound of someone stumbling. Then one of the doors opened just a crack. A grim, old face appeared in the opening.

The old fisherman pointed at DeKok.

"This is a policeman."

The knacker took off his spectacles and looked appraisingly at DeKok for several long seconds. The grim expression of his face disappeared.

"Come in," he said.

DeKok, followed by the old man, entered. The inside of the barn was a revelation. It was clean and neat. One wall, above a workbench was covered with saws, planes, chisels, hammers, augers and other carpenter's tools. All of an advanced age, but in excellent condition. In the center, at the end of a long chain, hung an old-fashioned storm lantern that threw a yellow light on a beautifully carved coffin lid. The coffin was almost completed.

The knacker pointed at the coffin.

"Griet of Lange Meindert was a big woman. Almost six feet. And then you have to keep in mind that the toes always stretch some."

"It's really a beautiful coffin," admired DeKok.

The old carpenter smiled, flattered by the compliment.

"Well, what do you want. It's her final home. Griet has always been a bit ostentatious. She'll be happy with this one."

DeKok found a low stool and lowered himself into a sitting position.

"This afternoon," he began, "I had a talk with the young doctor. He says that you're spreading rumors about him."

The carpenter peered at DeKok from over his glasses. His eyes sparkled.

"So, is that what he says?"

DeKok nodded convincingly.

"Yes. He wasn't at all pleased about you. He called you an old drunk who was happy whenever somebody died."

The knacker clamped his mouth shut. He was visibly upset. DeKok consciously fed the fire.

"He said that you're drunk as a skunk when you leave the house of the dear departed."

The old man bristled. He took a few steps in the direction of DeKok.

"You know why he says that?"

"Well?"

"Because he hates me."

"Really?"

The old carpenter nodded vehemently.

"Yes. I found him out, you see. He tried to get me drunk when young Talema died. Have-another-old-man, he kept repeating, come-on-have-another ... Well, I didn't care, I took. The bottle was there on the table, after all. And as soon as the first one was empty, he brought out another one." The man raised his hand and mimicked his own actions. "No, no, doctor, I said, no more. First I gotta do my work."

"Then what happened?"

"Well, then we lifted Tjeerd from the bed and placed him in the coffin. The doctor took the head and I took the feet." He paused and stared somberly at the dirt floor of the immaculate barn. "You see," he continued, "I just about put half the town in their coffins, but I've never had one with warm feet."

DeKok's mouth fell open in surprise.

"What!?"

"Warm feet! And when I mentioned it, he became furious."

* * *

They walked down the alley. The pregnant tones of a psalm followed them from the barn. The knacker had gone back to work.

DeKok nudged the fisherman.

"Did you know about the warm feet?"

"Yes, I'd heard about it."

"Why didn't you tell me?"

The man shrugged his shoulders.

"Because I don't believe it."

DeKok stopped in the middle of the street and stared at his companion.

"You don't believe it? The knacker is a pious man."

"So what. When I finish a bottle of *jenever*, my wife looks like a maid of eighteen."

"Isn't she?"

The old man cackled.

"She was seventy-three, last week."

* * *

"Tjeerd Talema?" asked the lady behind the counter and looked at DeKok. "Somebody from Amsterdam called about him earlier this week."

DeKok nodded agreeably.

"That was my colleague, Vledder."

She wrinkled her nose. DeKok found the expression enchanting.

"He wasn't very polite. Not friendly at all. He broke the connection without so much as a greeting."

DeKok smiled.

"I came special, all the way from Amsterdam, to apologize for that. You see, it was from shock. The surprise, really. We didn't know that Tjeerd had been dead for so long. We were under the impression that about six weeks ago he still had a cup of coffee in *The Beehive*."

"The department store?"

"Yes."

"Oh."

"Exactly. And we would like to know very much to whom Tjeerd was married."

"Was he married?"

DeKok grinned boyishly.

"Perhaps if you were to look in your records . . ."

"Oh, of course," answered the woman, utterly charmed by DeKok's grin, but unable to explain why this large, craggy, somewhat melancholy man had suddenly become so attractive. As she turned to comply, DeKok added:

"We would also very much like to know if anybody else has asked for information about Tjeerd. Perhaps a copy of a Birth Certificate, or a Death Certificate. Do you keep records of that?"

"Requests for copies from the files?"

"Yes."

"Of course, we do. I'll check."

She disappeared into another room.

DeKok sat down on a bench opposite the counter and prepared to wait. From bitter experience he knew that a search through the records could take a long time. He searched through his pockets and found a piece of hard candy. Thoughtfully he popped it in his mouth. He looked around. The interior seemed dark. There was no artificial light and the light that came through the high, stained-glass windows was diffused.

Suddenly the door opened. The man in the doorway looked at DeKok with surprise. It took a second or two before DeKok recognized the new visitor. Without the intimidating surgical jacket, dressed in street clothes, he looked a lot less formidable.

188

"Dr. Hoekstra . . . good morning." DeKok stood up and stretched out a welcoming hand. After a slight hesitation, the doctor came nearer and shook hands.

"Good morning, Inspector."

DeKok gave him a winning smile.

"Isn't that a pleasant coincidence. That we should happen to meet just now. Are you reporting a death?" It sounded ironic.

The young doctor did not react.

"You caught me off-balance yesterday," he said thoughtfully. "I had not expected your visit. It set me to thinking. Did you know that Tjeerd was married?"

DeKok shook his head.

"I didn't know . . . not until Ilona told me."

"Have you seen her?"

DeKok looked at him. His eyes were mocking.

"You didn't know?"

"No."

"Now, isn't that weird," teased DeKok. "I thought everybody knew everything about everybody else." He gestured vaguely, a nonchalant, careless movement. "I also visited the knacker," he continued conversationally. "His version of what happened differs markedly from your story. Apparently it wasn't so much *him* that wanted to get drunk, but *you* who wanted to get him drunk."

"You seem to attach an extraordinary amount of importance to village gossip."

DeKok narrowed his eyes and gave the other a penetrating look.

"Let's clear something up between us, Dr. Hoekstra." His tone had become sharp, incisive. "I'm not investigating village gossip, but a murder."

"Murder?"

189

"Yes. Tjeerd Talema was murdered. And murder, Dr. Hoekstra, *always* has my complete, professional attention."

The doctor lowered himself on the bench. His face was pale.

"Tjeerd . . . murdered?"

DeKok looked down at the younger man. He liked the young doctor. He took no pleasure in torturing him, but there was no other way. He had to know the truth.

"Yes. But *that* murder shouldn't concern you at all, my dear doctor," he said sarcastically. "Why should you be concerned, right? After all, your friend Tjeerd Talema died three years ago . . . as the result of a coronary."

The doctor rose. Without another word he staggered toward the door. DeKok watched him leave.

"In case you need me," he called after the disappearing figure, "Room 9, Warmoes Street, Amsterdam."

The lady called something from behind the counter. DeKok turned toward her and approached her.

"Wasn't that the young doctor?" she asked.

"Yes, that was the young doctor."

"What did he want?"

DeKok grinned broadly.

"That, my dear, I will ask him the next time I see him."

18

Vledder carefully balanced two steaming mugs of coffee in one hand while clutching a stack of papers with the other. Slowly he traversed the large, busy detective room of the old and renowned Warmoes Street Station. With a sigh of relief he placed both mugs on DeKok's desk and pushed one closer to his older colleague. He dumped the papers on his own desk, pulled out a chair, placed the chair next to DeKok's desk and took a careful, grateful sip from his coffee.

"So," he began, "now you're convinced that Tjeerd did *not* die three years ago."

DeKok smiled, slurped his coffee with comfortable enjoyment, oblivious to the stares of some of the other occupants of the room and looked at his young, eager assistant.

"He died ... officially."

"But not for real?"

"No, not for real. It was a sham."

Vledder moved impatiently in his chair.

"How was that possible?"

"Exactly the question I asked. How was it possible? Please keep in mind that this is only a theory. I have no hard facts to back it up. But I *do* have a number of important pointers."

He slurped again from his coffee. An uncivilized sound. Vledder never knew if it was done to annoy people, or if DeKok was truly not aware of what he was doing. It was peculiar, thought Vledder, he only slurped coffee. With everything else, DeKok's table manners were impeccable.

"At first I thought about a case of mistaken identity. What I mean is that I thought that the man we fished from the water had, for whatever reason, assumed Tjeerd's identity. That's the main reason I took Mabel's painting to Zoetekamp. When I got there, I displayed it in the taproom of the local hotel, the *Zoetekamp Arms*, and waited for results."

Vledder smirked in anticipation.

"Much to my surprise, the owner of the hotel, a certain Jauwkien, and her customers immediately identified the painting. That's Tjeerd, they said. There was no question that they were talking about the Tjeerd who apparently died three years ago."

Vledder's eyes sparkled.

"And there was your proof. No case of mistaken identity. The man we found and Tjeerd Talema from Zoetekamp were one and the same person."

"Exactly," responded DeKok. "But that was, of course, absurd. Nobody dies more than once. No matter what sort of explanation I tried to apply to the problem, there was really only one logical explanation. That was that Tjeerd could not possibly have died three years ago."

He scratched the back of his neck, reminiscing about what he had seen and heard.

"Believe me," he continued, "the grave stone was very impressive and convincing. But the text was the first clue, so to speak. It made me think. The text read: *He, who has conquered even death*... and that seemed a bit much. True, Zoetekamp can, with a certain justification, be called a stronghold of old-fashioned Calvinism. A text like that would not be strange. Not there. The obvious explanation is a reference to the Resurrection of Christ and the promised eternal life. The conquest of death. The old fisherman who was my guide was full of praise for the text. But he added that the young doctor was universally considered to be an atheist."

Vledder grinned.

"The citizens of Zoetekamp could explain the text one way, but that specific formulation was subject to a different interpretation as well."

DeKok nodded.

"Also, the young doctor played a peculiar role in this entire affair."

"How's that?"

"Not only did he take care of the stone ... and the text. Tjeerd Talema died in the doctor's house and ... the doctor allowed nobody near the corpse."

"What do you mean?"

"Yes, he even denied access to Ilona Kastanje, a friend of Tjeerd's youth, a woman who loved the deceased dearly. He would not let her see Tjeerd, dead or alive, despite the fact that she wanted that very much. The doctor considered it dangerous for her health."

A deep crease appeared in Vledder's forehead while he replaced his mug on the desk.

"Did *anybody* see the corpse?"

"Just the knacker."

"What's a knacker?"

DeKok smiled.

"A friendly old carpenter who makes beautifully carved coffins while praising the Lord loudly in psalms." He looked at Vledder's unbelieving face and added. "You don't have to look that way. It's a tradition in the village. There's no undertaker and the carpenter makes all the coffins, when there's a need. All made-to-measure, so to speak. He also seems to be an extremely devout man, a former precentor in church, and he sings psalms while he works."

"Really?"

"Really. But don't get the wrong idea. He also likes a drink now and then. Part of the tradition involves having a drink with the carpenter when he comes to measure the corpse and then again when he delivers the coffin."

Vledder leaned back in his chair. As far as the young inspector was concerned, DeKok could be talking about another planet. Nevertheless he listened carefully while DeKok explained.

"And there's the rub," sighed DeKok after a while. "The young doctor stated that he wanted to break the carpenter of his habit in the case of Tjeerd's death. He refused to offer him a drink. But when I discussed that with the knacker, he was highly indignant. According to the old carpenter, the doctor had tried to get him drunk. He stated as a matter of fact that they had not placed Tjeerd in the coffin until the carpenter had finished a bottle."

"A whole bottle?"

"Yes, it's a wonder he was still on his feet, let alone capable of helping to lift Tjeerd into the coffin."

"Dead Tjeerd?"

"No, I don't think so. You see, that's one of the problems. The doctor and the knacker quarreled."

"Quarreled? What about?"

DeKok grinned.

"The old carpenter declared ... mind you, this after a whole bottle of *jenever* ... that Tjeerd still had warm feet."

"Warm feet?" Vledder burst out laughing. After a moment he controlled himself and asked: "Then what?"

"The doctor became very angry and chased the carpenter from the house. Ever since that day, the one is spreading gossip about the other and vice versa."

Vledder's face looked serious.

"Still," he said, "I can't help but wonder about those warm feet. If your theory is in accordance with the facts ... in that case, despite a whole bottle of booze, the observation of the knacker ..." He groped for words. "You ... you must be right. Tjeerd wasn't dead. He was acting the part of a corpse."

"But could not control the temperature of his feet," concluded DeKok.

Vledder grinned softly to himself.

"No wonder the doctor was furious. His entire plan was on the brink of failure."

DeKok bit his lower lip, drained the last of his coffee and thoughtfully replaced the mug on the desk.

"And that's what bothers me more than anything."

"What?" asked Vledder.

"The plan. I mean, what could possibly be gained by having Tjeerd die officially, for the record. Just think about the risk for *both* men. The doctor especially will have to pay a severe penalty. He not only risked jail, but a forged Death Certificate might cost him his license to practice."

"You think so?"

DeKok nodded.

"Most certainly. A doctor who signs false, or forged Death Certificates cannot be tolerated by our society. The trustworthiness of the physician is one of the cornerstones of our civilization."

Vledder gave him a mocking glance. He never knew whether to believe DeKok at such moments.

"Nice words," he said finally.

DeKok nodded. His face was serious.

"I mean it. It would be close to anarchy if every doctor was allowed to just write Death Certificates at will."

"Is he a good physician?"

"I'm hardly in a position to judge. But, despite the gossip, he seems to have a lot of faithful patients."

Vledder looked searchingly at his older colleague. He had heard a certain undertone in DeKok's voice, a tone he had heard before.

"Are you going to expose him?"

DeKok raked his fingers through his hair.

"That's a difficult question. If I inform the Judge-Advocate of the facts as I know them and the coincidences I suspect, I'm almost sure we'll get an order for exhumation. That would certainly provide adequate proof and expose the doctor. No question about that."

"What do you expect to find in the coffin?"

"Sand, or rocks, whatever."

Vledder leaned closer toward his mentor.

"You . . . you don't really feel like it, do you?"

DeKok smiled sadly.

"What *are* you talking about?"

"Exhumation . . . the doctor's arrest."

DeKok rose from behind his desk and started to pace up and down between the desks. After a while he stopped and looked down on Vledder, who had remained seated.

"We just don't know enough about the motives . . . the whys and the wherefores. Why the masquerade? Tjeerd and

Dirk Hoekstra were friends and I was under the impression that this friendship meant a lot to the young doctor. He was genuinely shocked when I told him that Tjeerd had been murdered. Also, I'm almost certain that the unfinished letter found by Sylvia was intended for the doctor."

Vledder looked up at him, confusion on his face.

"But that would mean that he knows all about the motives for the murder."

"Why?"

"From the content of the letter it's obvious that the intended recipient was familiar with everything."

DeKok shook his head.

"I believe you're mistaken. You're not thinking straight. The person to whom the letter was addressed knew Tjeerd's plans. To that extent he, or she, was aware of everything. But we can safely assume that Tjeerd's plans did *not* include his own murder. That would be too silly. The murder was unexpected, unforeseen. Therefore it would be precipitous to assume that the doctor would be aware of the motive for murder."

Vledder pressed his lips togethers. As usual, he had been too enthusiastic, too soon. He had to correct the tendency to jump to conclusions. He felt that DeKok's use of the word 'precipitous' was justified. But a stubborn streak made him persist.

"Still," he tried, annoyed, "I'm convinced that the motive for Tjeerd's murder was connected with his plans." He stood up, leaned over and fished a piece of paper from the pile he had dumped on his desk earlier. "While you were in Zoetekamp," he continued, "I went over everything again and again."

He held up the paper and showed it to DeKok.

"Here, look at the text. Tjeerd wrote his friend: . . . *I've reached the end of my odyssey. I have found her* . . . His odyssey, his search, must have been related to a search for *her!* And now that he had found her, he was at the end of his search. Simple, right?"

DeKok nodded resignedly.

"Very simple."

"And now the next sentence: . . . *and you know what that means* . . . To me it means he had plans . . . plans related to the woman for whom he was searching. Plans that his friend knew about."

"Exactly."

"Then he writes: . . . *It's strange, but I'm neither happy, nor bitter. My heart is empty* . . . I'm thinking here about the remark made by Uncle Louis of the boarding house. He told us that he found Tjeerd disillusioned."

Vledder looked at the gray sleuth with a certain amount of triumph in his expression. DeKok looked at him without expression.

"Well," concluded Vledder, "when you put it all together, you get a picture of a man, initially embittered and disappointed, who is engaged in a fanatical search for a woman, but who, after he's found her, feels his bitterness less and wonders about the meaning of it all."

"A nice analysis, but what does it mean."

"Nothing yet, but it raises three questions: Why the original embitterment and disappointment? Who was the woman he was looking for . . . and found? And what did he want with her? If the letter was indeed meant for your doctor up North, he should be able to answer all three of those questions."

DeKok's face was transformed by a friendly grin.

"I don't need the doctor for that," he smiled.

"No?"

DeKok shook his head.

"No, because I can answer the last two questions right now: The woman was Alida Somers and the plan was ... murder."

19

Vledder looked at him in astonishment.

"How did you arrive at that conclusion?"

DeKok grinned his boyish grin.

"It's not all that mysterious. Ilona told me that Tjeerd had married about eighteen months before his so-called demise. He wrote her a letter about finding his 'great love' and asked for understanding. She wrote back that she had all the understanding in the world and promptly became heartsick with sorrow."

"Poor thing."

"Yes. Anyway, later she heard that Tjeerd had married the 'love-of-his-life'. But the strange thing is that, with the exception of Ilona and the young doctor, nobody in Zoetekamp seemed to have known about the wife. Nobody had seen her. She didn't even attend the funeral."

DeKok paused and gave Vledder a pleading look.

"How about another cup of coffee?"

Vledder shook his head decisively.

"First I want to know more."

DeKok smiled.

"All right already. I went to the Zoetekamp Town Hall. Fortunately the lady behind the counter was the patient type.

I must have tried her patience some. I had a lot of questions. According to the records, it seemed that Tjeerd had indeed married one Alida Somers, approximately eighteen months before his official death. She was a Belgian lady."

"Where was the ceremony?"

"In Utrecht."

Vledder looked thoughtfully into the distance.

"Alida Somers . . . the name means nothing to me."

"Me neither. So far this is the first time we have stumbled on that name."

Vledder glanced at his colleague.

"But you said that she was the woman Tjeerd was looking for . . . and found."

DeKok nodded slowly, glanced longingly at his empty coffee mug and then at Vledder.

"That's what I said," he sighed.

Vledder swallowed.

"And you also said that Tjeerd planned to kill her."

"Indeed, I said that as well."

Vledder showed his impatience.

"Well then . . . out with it."

"Coffee first."

Vledder capitulated. He stood up, grabbed the mugs from the desk and walked over to the percolator near the small water fountain. He poured, aimed three cubes of sugar at DeKok's mug and returned to the desk. He pushed one mug closer to his old friend.

"This is nothing but blackmail, you know that."

The gray sleuth laughed as he shook his head.

"Not really," he said, "just respect for an older colleague. Besides," he teased, "coffee tastes so much better when someone else pours it for you."

Vledder growled something unintelligible.

DeKok stretched out a hand in a reconciling gesture.

"Actually," he soothed, "with a little thought you would have been able to figure it out for yourself."

"How?"

"Think, my boy, think. Tjeerd writes Ilona about his 'great love', but barely eighteen months later the so-called 'great love' can't even be bothered to attend the funeral of her husband."

"Maybe she didn't know he was dead?"

DeKok pressed his lips together and smiled grimly.

"She knew," he said sharply. "She knew all right, because less than a month later she wrote to Zoetekamp and requested a copy of the Death Certificate. The return address was *Hotel International* in Zurich."

"Zurich, Switzerland?"

"Yes. I called the police in Zurich. They could only tell me that she had stayed in the hotel for several days. She was registered as Alida Somers, Dutch, widow of T. Talema."

Vledder was lost in thought. His face became expressionless and a deep crease appeared on his forehead. DeKok slurped from his coffee.

"Now I understand," exclaimed Vledder after a long pause. "You think that Alida didn't come to Zoetekamp with her husband and didn't attend the funeral because she knew in advance what was going to happen."

DeKok nodded encouragingly at his younger colleague.

"Excellent, Dick, really excellent. Apparently she *knew* that Tjeerd's only reason for going to Zoetekamp was to die officially, for the form, so to speak."

Vledder chortled.

"She didn't feel much like attending the funeral of a sandbag."

DeKok scratched behind his ear.

"Actually," he said thoughtfully, "I believe she stayed away from Zoetekamp in order to, as much as possible, limit the number of people who knew her as Tjeerd's wife."

"But," objected Vledder, "that still doesn't explain why Tjeerd would want to kill her."

DeKok shook his head.

"No, it doesn't. I never said I knew *why* he wanted to kill her. I only said that he *wanted* to kill her. Certainly he seriously contemplated the subject of murder. Let me remind you of the remark that Sylvia remembers so vividly: *Can a dead person commit murder?* You found it a stupid question. But look at it in the light of what we know, or suspect, now. Then it starts to make sense. Tjeerd was talking about himself. He was wondering if, as somebody who had been officially declared dead, he could be held responsibly under the Law. Remember, Tjeerd was a lawyer."

Vledder nodded understanding.

"Yes, of course, and he considered the possibility of being arrested for the crime, contemplated his defense, more or less."

DeKok took a deep breath.

"Indeed, a pretty judicial puzzle. The sort of thing lawyers just love to split hairs over. But the thought of murder remained central to his thinking. And then we come to the question: Who was Tjeerd's intended victim?"

DeKok paused, slurped his coffee. Vledder waited for him to continue.

"The answer to the last question," said DeKok, "is not all that difficult. There were only three main characters in what we could call *the Zoetekamp Games*: Tjeerd, the 'corpse', Dr. Hoekstra, who declared him dead and Alida Somers, the wife who needed an official copy from the Town

Records. We know, from the incomplete letter, that Tjeerd had no feelings of hate toward the doctor. He wrote to him as to a friend and reported that he had found her ... Alida Somers, his 'great love', but also the woman who had embittered him, who had disillusioned him."

They both remained silent. The silence was almost a palpable presence between them. It was as if Tjeerd was again confronted with the question about the sense of it all. What had been his ultimate answer? What was he doing, late at night on the fourteenth of March? Was he on his way to kill the woman who had disappointed him, or ... ?

Vledder was the first to break the silence.

"I haven't found Mabel yet," he said slowly.

"And what about Robert Hoveneer?"

Vledder snorted contemptuously.

"Drunk."

Before DeKok repeated the question, Vledder was treated to an extremely fine performance by DeKok's eyebrows.

"Drunk?" asked DeKok.

Vledder nodded, after tearing his gaze away from DeKok's forehead.

"Twelve hours a day. The other twelve hours he spends sleeping it off. Do you need him?"

"Maybe."

"He's easy to find. When he isn't sleeping it off, he's in that little bar on the Singel,* near Tower Locks."

"How long has that been going on?"

"The drinking?"

---

* Singel, another word for *gracht* (canal). Singel generally indicates a wider, more grandiose canal, or a street formed by filling the canal. Most canals have qualifiers (names), i.e. *Brewers* Canal. This is simply *the* Singel, a well-known Amsterdam landmark.

"Yes."

"Practically from the moment that you last talked to him."

"Have you had any personal contact with him?"

"No, I'll leave that to you."

"What about the rest of the family?"

Vledder smiled.

"Uncle Charles complains all the time, about everything and nothing. But especially about the reporters who, so he claims, have sullied his good name. His wife tells him it's his own fault for taking in Mabel. That was the start of all their problems."

DeKok gave him a long, hard look.

"How do you know all that?"

Vledder winked.

"I speak regularly with the maid. She keeps me pretty well informed."

"Oh?" There was just a hint of disapproval in DeKok's voice.

"Nothing untoward," Vledder hastened to explain. "I walk her home, or buy her a cup of coffee. She's a dear girl and I wouldn't dream of taking advantage of her. But she *does* like to talk."

DeKok rubbed the bridge of his nose with a little finger.

"One of these days, Dick," he remarked off-handedly, "you'll be a great detective."

Vledder blushed. He could not have said himself whether it was because of the implied praise, or the slight undertone of sarcasm in DeKok's voice.

"I really haven't been wasting my time while you were away," he protested moodily. "I mean, I didn't spent all my time with the maid. I've also been looking for Mabel

Paddington. I've asked all her friends at the Academy. Nobody could tell me anything."

"Maybe she went back to England."

Vledder shook his head.

"No, I checked. She isn't in England, either. At least, she's not with her parents, or with friends there. Anyway, her passport is still at the Hoveneer residence."

DeKok nodded.

"That doesn't mean much, what with the EEC and all. But a British subject would be less inclined to travel without a passport than anyone else in Europe. It's probably safe to assume that she's still in Amsterdam. I still think we have to find her and as soon as possible. In the beginning I wasn't too worried about her disappearance, but that's changing as time progresses. I'm more concerned now than I was."

Vledder looked at him, confusion on his face.

"You think that she . . ."

"What?"

"That she killed Tjeerd?"

DeKok did not answer at once. Thoughtfully he stared at nothing at all. Then he drained the last of his second mug of coffee.

"Well, I tell you, Dick," he began, slowly, hesitatingly. "Mabel Paddington has been a riddle to me from the beginning. The same day that we fished the corpse from the Brewers Canal, she showed up with that painting. She asked if I was in charge of the drowned person. When I admitted that, she offered information. *I went with him, we dated, we flirted, we loved each other*, she said. That was odd, to say the least. Because how did she know in advance, without any further information that the victim was her friend? And why was she carrying the portrait? There had been a description in the paper, true, but at the time Mabel visited me she could have had no reason to suspect that the corpse was that of her Marcel. As a matter of fact, she could not reasonably have missed him already."

"How's that?"

"Well, if Marcel, as he called himself to her, had been gone for a long period of time and she had *then* seen a description in the paper, her behavior would have been reasonable, within the norm to be expected. But she had talked to him only the day before. Just sweet nothings. There was absolutely no indication of a threat, of an impending disaster."

Vledder looked serious.

"Yes, you're right, in retrospect it *does* seem suspicious that she came to see you so quickly."

DeKok nodded.

"But what astonished me the most was her reaction to the news that her friend had been murdered. She immediately supplied the suspect."

"Robert Hoveneer."

"Yes, complete with motive and all. And when we did not follow up fast enough to suit her, she orchestrated that incredible performance in the Chapel."

Vledder thought deeply.

"Could she really be convinced that Robert is the killer?"

DeKok made a nonchalant gesture.

"There are two possibilities. Either she has tried from the beginning to steer our investigations into the wrong direction, or she has seen, or heard, something that makes her certain that Robert is the killer."

Vledder raised a finger in the air. The gesture looked familiar to DeKok, but he was not consciously aware that it was one of his own habits.

"But," said Vledder, "the fact that she knew about the location of the wound, should certainly indicate that she knows *something* about the whole affair."

DeKok rose slowly from his chair. He glanced at his watch. It was almost midnight. Slowly he ambled over to the coat rack and donned his ridiculous little hat.

"You're hitting the road?"

"Yes."

"Where?"

"To the Singel. To the bar near Tower Locks. If I happen to meet Robert Hoveneer when he leaves the bar, I'll arrest him."

Vledder looked puzzled.

"Arrest?" he asked.

"Yes."

"For murder?"

DeKok pushed his hat down deep on his forehead. There was a wicked gleam in his eyes.

"No," he answered, "for intoxication in public."

20

"You look like hell."

Robert Hoveneer looked at the gray sleuth and grinned a drunkard's grin.

"What did you expect?"

DeKok shrugged his shoulders.

"It's just sad to see a man lose his self-respect this way."

Robert snorted. The walk to the station had done a lot to sober him up.

"Have you ever been accused? Accused of murder by the only woman you've ever loved? *That's* sad. And it's even sadder when afterward you discover ..." He did not complete the sentence, but looked at DeKok with a stupefied expression on his face. "Am I under arrest?"

"About half an hour ago," DeKok answered evenly.

"For murder?"

The Inspector smiled.

"Is that possible?" he asked, evading the question. "Can I arrest you for murder? You've maintained all along you had nothing to do with Marcel's killing. Changed your mind?"

Young Hoveneer half rose from his chair and leaned in the direction of DeKok.

"I know it," he cried. "I know I've got nothing to do with it." He slammed his fist against his chest. "I know it right here! But who else knows?" He covered his face with his hands. "My God, if this goes on much longer, even I'll believe I did it." He sank back in his chair and rubbed the back of his hand along dry lips. "May I have a glass of water?"

DeKok went to the water fountain and poured a glass of water. He looked at his suspect through the mirror above the tap. That boy just wasn't prepared to deal with stress, he thought. He turned and placed the glass in front of Robert.

"I would like to offer you a beer, but I don't have any."

Robert smiled weakly.

"I've talked to a lot of people, Inspector," he said. "You'd be amazed how many people want to talk to you when you offer them a drink. The more drinks, the more they talk. You want to know what they tell me?"

"Well?"

"They say, Inspector DeKok, that you are a very clever man . . . that, no matter what, you always get your man. Maybe that's why it's better if I put all my cards on the table." He pulled his tie loose and rubbed the inside of his collar. "I've been thinking, Inspector. I've been thinking so long that it makes me sick."

"And?"

Hoveneer placed an index finger next to his nose in a conspiratorial gesture.

"Now, you must listen carefully. Mabel says that I killed Marcel."

"That's what she says."

"Exactly. And Mabel isn't crazy. I mean, she isn't the sort of girl who just makes statements like that for the hell of it."

"I presume so."

The young man gestured wildly around.

"Well, her conclusions must be based on some fact, you agree? She must have heard, or seen, something."

DeKok looked at him evenly.

"You sound remarkably clear for a man who's filled himself to the gills with booze."

Robert Hoveneer tapped the side of his head with a crooked finger.

"Make no mistake about it," he grinned lop-sidedly, "I know what I'm saying. Don't think that I'm being frank to please you. I just don't want to be the fall-guy. That's all."

DeKok's eyebrows rippled briefly, but Hoveneer did not notice. He grinned in the direction of the desk-top, a cunning look in his eyes.

"Yes, something underhanded is going on. Marcel wasn't killed for nothing. I mean, you don't bash in someone's skull just because you don't like his face. The man who killed Marcel knew exactly what he was doing."

"Man?"

* * *

Hoveneer tore his gaze away from the desk-top and looked up in surprise.

"You do listen carefully," he admired. "I said man . . . and I mean man." He picked up the glass of water and drank almost half of it in one, long swallow. Then he continued.

"That crazy portrait that Mabel painted . . . that was good, it was so good that even you were upset by it." He nodded toward DeKok as if to reassure him. "Yes, you can hardly deny that. It upset you and you immediately came to a conclusion . . . the same conclusion at which I arrived . . .

several days later. Mabel could only have painted that portrait as accurately as she did . . . if she had seen Marcel when he was dead."

DeKok raked his fingers through his hair.

"It seems a logical conclusion," he admitted.

Robert Hoveneer removed his strange glasses, pulled a shirttail from his pants and wiped the glasses with it.

"You *know*," he said calmly, but with emphasis, "that it is the *right* conclusion. Mabel Paddington saw Marcel when he was dead and . . . she saw the killer."

"What!?"

"She saw the killer," repeated Robert calmly and without batting an eye. "She saw the killer, but misidentified him. She thought she saw me, maybe because she *wanted* to see me. But she saw the only person who resembles me somewhat, especially from a distance . . . Uncle Charles."

* * *

"Did you take him home?"

Vledder took off his coat.

"Yes," he sighed, "I took him to the Emperor's Canal and dragged him out of the car. I used his key to open the door for him and I even helped him up the stairs to his room."

"Very good."

Vledder snorted.

"I looked like a man-servant."

"That's all right," grinned DeKok. "You're a cop. You're supposed to serve the public. But apart from that, it was no more than our duty to make sure he would get home safe and sound. You can't arrest a man for being intoxicated and then let him walk out after an hour. That would have been bad manners."

Vledder growled.

"He wasn't all that drunk. I thought he said some very intelligent things. I've wondered from the beginning why Mabel was so eager to accuse Robert. I think his explanation is very plausible. I think maybe we should ask Uncle Charles a few hard questions."

DeKok stood up.

"Mind you," he said, one hand on the back of his chair, "I would take Robert's thoughts that the murder has something to do with his Uncle's financial machinations with a large dose of salt. Charles is a stock broker. He and Marcel hardly moved in the same circles."

"You don't believe Robert?"

"Partly, maybe. It's entirely possible that Charles killed Marcel, or Tjeerd, as we should properly call him. It's even possible that Mabel witnessed the deed from a distance, even if I don't understand how. But believe you me, Tjeerd wasn't killed because of Charles' financial shenanigans. He was killed because of something that happened in Zoete-kamp."

Vledder looked up at him.

"But what's the connection between the Hoveneers and Zoetekamp?"

The older man rubbed the corners of his eyes with a tired movement.

"A good question," he answered lethargically. "We should sleep on that." He pointed at the clock over the door. "It's two o'clock already. Tomorrow you draft Inspector Dijk. Between the two of you, you try to discover Mabel's whereabouts. She must be somewhere. It's about time she tells us what she has seen."

"And what about you?"

"I'm going to Utrecht."

"Whatever for?"

"Tjeerd Talema married Alida Somers, remember?"

"But you can do that by telephone!"

DeKok shook his head.

"No, I've got to have absolute proof. I already have confirmation. They married on the sixteenth of September. I requested a copy of the Marriage Certificate. It came over one of those machines." He pointed disdainfully at a fax machine, unwilling to admit that it had its uses.

"Then why are you going?"

"Ilona Kastanje used to write letters to her Tjeerd when he was in Utrecht."

Vledder's face cleared up.

"And she gave you the address to which she wrote?"

DeKok nodded wearily.

"Right. And I'm going in the hope," he said, unable to keep a slight mockery out of his voice, "that I may meet some people who remember the sublime happiness of the young couple."

It sounded cynical, but DeKok had been a cop for a long time and he was tired. Vledder understood.

* * *

DeKok strolled through the Red Light District on the way home. His hands were buried in the pockets of his raincoat and he sucked contently on a piece of candy. He had refused Vledder's offer to drop him off by car. He liked to walk. And experience had taught him that his thoughts could be ordered better if he walked. And he needed the time, the respite between a long day and the rest his body needed. If he went home by car, his thoughts would still be in turmoil when he got there. It was too quick, it left no time for reflection and sleep would elude him.

The day had started early, in Zoetekamp. Then the ferry back to Amsterdam. The water had been rough. The tamed lake had shown aspirations of returning to its primeval state, of turning back into the wild Inland Sea of earlier days, so eloquently described by Jan De Hartog in *The Lost Sea*. Not until the ship slid between the long dikes that marked the approach to Amsterdam, had he been able to rest a little. Then catching up with the paperwork he detested and the long conference with Vledder. Finally the late-night "arrest" of Robert Hoveneer. It had been a long day.

The case had also drained him. It was about a week ago that the corpse had first been discovered. A lot had happened since. The debilitating search for the man's identity had taken a lot of time, had muddied the waters, confused the background. But despite all that, he felt that he was getting close. If tomorrow in Utrecht ...

His musings were suddenly interrupted by the feeling that he was being followed. He turned into a dark alley, away from the bars and brothels that produced a lot of noise, even at this late hour. In the relatively quiet alley he listened carefully, without changing his pace. He could hear footsteps and they were close. He turned another corner, into Whirlpool Alley. He knew the quarter like no other. Every alley, every portico, every door. He reached a small square, not much more than a widening of the narrow street. A marble fountain was incongruously placed in the center. With a quick burst of speed he reached the fountain and melded into the shadows. He watched a man emerge from the end of the street he had just left. As he passed a lit beer sign, he immediately recognized his pursuer. The man approached carefully, cautiously. Next to the fountain he stopped and looked around, confused, uncertain. DeKok slowly straightened out from his crouched position. He approached his pursuer with a wide smile on his face.

"Good morning, Dr. Hoekstra."

21

"All of a sudden you had disappeared."

DeKok smiled.

"You shouldn't try to shadow a cop."

Hoekstra looked serious.

"I wanted to talk to you. I wanted to visit you at home, but I didn't know the address. I asked the desk-sergeant how I could reach you and he told me you were still in the station."

"Then why didn't you come up?"

The young doctor smiled shyly.

"I waited outside for you. I didn't want to meet you in the police station. I wanted to talk to you as a human being ... not as a cop."

DeKok looked at him evenly.

"I *am* a human being ... and a cop."

Hoekstra sighed.

"I had no intention of offending you. But it's a matter of feeling, of atmosphere. If I had visited you in the station, my visit would have been, or so I feel it, would have been official. And I want to avoid the official aspects as much as possible."

DeKok nodded wisely.

"You want an informal conversation, off the record."

"Something like that, yes."

"Let's walk in the direction of my home. I don't get all that much sleep as it is."

As they walked on in silence, DeKok glanced at the doctor from time to time. Hoekstra looked neither left, nor right and seemed under a considerable amount of nervous tension. Apparently he had difficulty deciding on an opening. Finally, without looking at DeKok, he asked a question.

"When will you close the case?"

"After I've arrested Tjeerd's murderer."

"Will that take long?"

DeKok slowly shook his head.

"It's a matter of proof."

"And you have no proof?"

"Not sufficient."

"Do you know the background?"

DeKok smiled without mirth.

"I know what happened in Zoetekamp. When I inform the Judge-Advocate, he'll no doubt order an exhumation."

"And what does that mean?"

"Your arrest."

"You haven't informed him?"

"No, I've not even told my Chief, the Commissaris. Sometimes I'm a bit careless about details."

The doctor doubted that DeKok was careless about details, but he mulled over what he had heard. He had trouble understanding DeKok's motives. Was the old detective playing a game of cat and mouse?

"How did Tjeerd die?"

"Somebody bashed in his head."

"Where?"

DeKok pointed ahead of him.

"Somewhere around here, I expect. They threw his body in the canal."

Hoekstra's face fell. His voice sounded sad.

"Poor Tjeerd. He had such great expectations."

"Was she beautiful?"

"Who?"

"Alida Somers."

"I never met her personally. I only know her through Tjeerd's descriptions. He was spell-bound by her ... couldn't stop talking about her. According to him she was the most beautiful woman of all time. Helen of Troy was a hag compared to her. He described her as a woman to ... to ..."

"... to die for," completed DeKok.

The doctor looked at DeKok for the first time since they had met at the fountain.

"That sounds a bit cynical. Tjeerd died *twice* for her."

They remained silent after that. They walked on for a long time without uttering a word. DeKok stopped on one of the bridges across the Brewers Canal. He leaned his arms on the railing and stared into the water. The canals were being drained and recycled. A strong current emerged from underneath the bridge and washed around the bollards that protected the entrance to the bridge from careless skippers. He turned away from the sluiced water and looked at the doctor.

"The masquerade in Zoetekamp would have been impossible without your cooperation."

"I know."

"What possessed you to be persuaded?"

Hoekstra shrugged his shoulders.

"Friendship and greed . . . or greed and friendship. Take your pick, I don't know which was more important. Not any more."

DeKok waited. There was more, he felt. He was right.

"My parents weren't rich, Mr. DeKok. They made a lot of sacrifices to enable me to study. Of course, I'm grateful for that. Will always be grateful. But if you want to take over a practice and you have no money . . ." He did not finish the sentence.

Again DeKok waited patiently. The doctor swallowed and sighed. Then he went on.

"At first I didn't even know what I had started. Did not think about the consequences. When Tjeerd first approached me with the idea, I thought it funny. A student's prank. It brought back memories. Give society a kick in the teeth, make it sit up and take notice. Strike a blow for freedom. I know, it sounds silly now, stupid. But I didn't look at it that way in the beginning. Later, yes. I've been living on the edge for years now. Add to that the ever present gossip in the village. Never a let-up. I persisted because of Tjeerd. Otherwise I would have made a clean breast of it long ago. If it hadn't been for Tjeerd I would have informed the authorities."

"How bourgeois."

The young man reacted vehemently. The first showing of passion.

"Are remorse and middle class morality mutually exclusive?"

"You're a doctor by choice? You had a calling?" asked DeKok.

The young man seemed momentarily nonplussed by the non-sequitur. Then a sad expression filled his face.

"No, calling is too big a word. I'm no idealist and I didn't hear 'voices'. But I knew what I wanted when I decided on medicine. It was a conscious choice."

DeKok nodded, apparently satisfied with the answer.

"There are countries in this world," he began softly, hesitatingly, "so-called third-world countries that have a chronic shortage of physicians." He paused and looked at the doctor, estimating the effect of his words. "Most of those countries are not members of Interpol, have no extradition agreements."

Hoekstra swallowed. His adam's apple bobbed up and down. He had difficulty speaking.

"You m-mean," he stammered finally.

"I mean," said DeKok sharply, "that nobody benefits if you go to jail."

Hoekstra nodded pensively.

"How much time do I have?"

"Two days."

"And then?"

"Then I'll try to arrest you."

DeKok pushed himself away from the railing against which he had been leaning and walked towards the opposite quay of the Brewers Canal. Near the edge of the water he stopped and pointed.

"This is where we found him."

"Tjeerd?"

"Yes, about a week ago."

The doctor stared into the water that still swirled around under the impetus of the huge pumps at the far side of Amsterdam. The current had created an eddy in the corner, near the bridge. A few planks and a rotted mattress twirled around, unable to get into the main stream. After a while he turned around, a determined look on his face.

"I was his friend . . . What will you do with his killer?"

* * *

"You take pictures at Town Hall?"

The man behind the counter peered at DeKok over his glasses.

"May I ask who you are?"

"But of course. My name is DeKok . . . with kay-oh-kay. I'm a Police Inspector."

"From Utrecht?"

"No, Amsterdam. Warmoes Street station."

The man looked weary.

"A well-known address. Homicide?"

"Yes," answered DeKok curtly.

"What can I do for you?"

"Do you make pictures of every bridal couple. Even without a commission?"

The man nodded calmly.

"It's a gamble, sometimes. Some take them and some don't. Of course, a lot of people have their own photographer."

"Do you keep all the pictures you take?"

"Yes."

"How long?"

"About thirteen years."

"Thirteen years?"

The man laughed at DeKok's surprised face.

"Yes, I often get requests for the original wedding pictures on the occasion of the Copper Wedding

Anniversaries"*

DeKok nodded understanding.

"About three and a half years ago, on the sixteenth of September, Tjeerd Talema married one Alida Somers, here in Town Hall. I wonder if you have pictures of that wedding."

The photographer frowned.

"What was the name of the couple?"

"Talema-Somers."

"Talema-Somers," repeated the man, surprise in his voice.

"Yes, is something the matter?"

"Yes, no, there seems to be a lot of interest for that couple, all of a sudden."

"How's that?"

The man smiled.

"You're the third."

"What?"

"Yes, two different women have asked for the same pictures."

"*Two* women?"

The photographer sighed.

"About three days ago," he began resignedly, "a young woman appeared . . . just a moment." He turned around and took a large brown envelope from a shelf behind him. " . . . a certain Miss M. Paddington, 57 Cat's Mews in Amsterdam."

"Paddington?"

"Yes. She asked for the pictures of the Talema-Somers wedding. I told her I had to search for the negatives and that she could pick up the pictures in a few days."

---

* Wedding Anniversaries generally celebrated in Holland: twelve and a half years (copper), twenty five years (silver), fifty years (gold) and seventy five years (diamond).

"Then what?"

"She paid in advance, asked me to send them and left. The next day another woman appeared and asked if I had saved the negatives from the Talema-Somers wedding. I told her I had and I added that I happened to have been looking for them, because somebody else had asked for them. The woman was highly surprised and asked who else was interested in the pictures."

DeKok stared at the photographer with wide open eyes.

"Then what," he asked, anxiety in his voice, "did you give the second woman Miss Paddington's address?"

"Yes," answered the man in a small voice, "I did."

DeKok clapped his hand to his face. For just an instant he seemed undecided, then he ripped the envelope from the photographer's hand and ran out the door.

He was back within seconds. The photographer looked at him with open mouth.

"Where is your telephone?" panted DeKok, "It's a matter of life or death."

22

Inspector Vledder stared somberly at the inanimate body of Mabel Paddington.

After the urgent phone call from DeKok, he and Dijk had driven to Cat's Mews at breakneck speed, sirens blaring, lights flashing. DeKok had called it a matter of life or death and DeKok never exaggerated. Even before the car had come to a complete stop, Dijk had jumped from the car and ran up the stairs, two, three steps at a time. Vledder had followed close behind.

She was spread out on the floor of the small room, not far from the door, a red scarf around her neck. She looked almost peaceful. There were no signs of force, no signs of a fight. The cloud of long, chestnut hair covered her face.

Vledder leaned over her and pushed some of the hair out of the way. She had been strangled. Without a doubt. And it had happened quickly with determined force. The victim had been dead before she had realized what was happening. Inevitably. There had been hardly any struggle, no defence. The red scarf which cut deeply into the neck had immediately blocked all oxygen to the brain.

Vledder placed the back of his hand against the girl's cheek. The body was cold. He took a small mirror from his pocket and held it before the mouth. The glass remained clean, did not cloud over.

Slowly he rose.

"We didn't have to be in such a hurry," he said, shaking his head. "She was already beyond help. Please go downstairs and call the *herd*."

Robert Antoine Dijk looked briefly at Vledder. As did everyone else on the force, Dijk knew that *Thundering Herd* was DeKok's special name for the battery of fingerprint experts, photographers, forensic people and other, assorted specialists who were always called in a murder case. He did not know that Vledder had started to use the same term. He took a last glance at the corpse.

"What a beautiful girl," whispered Dijk. "Really, almost too beautiful."

"You mean too beautiful to get killed?" Vledder's voice was brusque in a forlorn attempt to hide his emotions. He knew how his colleague felt. He felt the same.

"Yes, something like that," answered Dijk.

"Take it from me. Beautiful women are ten times more likely to get killed than ugly ones." He pointed at the door. "Please hurry, perhaps we'll have time to look around ourselves before the *herd* arrives."

Dijk ran down the stairs.

Vledder allowed his gaze to travel through the room. It was sparsely furnished. Almost poorly. A table next to the sink served as a counter. A camp stove on the makeshift counter supported a small saucepan which contained the remains of a canned meal.

So, thought Vledder, this had been Mabel's hideout for the last few days. Why? Who was she hiding from? How had DeKok discovered the address? In Utrecht? Vledder rubbed his chin. Questions seemed to overwhelm him. Who had killed her? He took a few paces to one side and looked at her from a different angle. Suddenly something on the floor caught his attention. Close to the head, something glistened between the chestnut hair. It looked like metal. He lowered himself to one knee and used a ballpoint pen to move the object carefully into the open.

Dijk had returned. He looked at Vledder from the door opening.

"Find something?"

Vledder nodded.

"A lighter . . . a nice one. Looks like silver."

"From the killer?"

"Maybe . . . you have a magnifying glass on you?"

Dijk searched his pockets and produced a jeweler's loupe.

"Here."

Vledder accepted the instrument, screwed it into one eye and leaned over the lighter. Dijk held his breath.

"Anything on it?"

"Yes, letters, initials. They're a bit worn, but they can be read."

"What sort of letters?"

"R.H."

Vledder slowly rose to his feet. There was a determined, angry look on his face.

"R.H.," he said bitterly. "The initials stand for Robert Hoveneer."

* * *

DeKok listened carefully to the reports by Vledder and Dijk. They were sitting in one of the interrogation rooms in order to escape the noise and turmoil in the large detective room upstairs. First Vledder and then Dijk related what they had found and seen in the small room at Cat's Mews.

"She was strangled," said DeKok.

Vledder nodded.

"With a red scarf. She must have been attacked from behind. The free ends of the scarf were on her back."

DeKok rubbed the bridge of his nose with a little finger. He looked from one to the other of the young detectives.

"And now you want to arrest Robert Hoveneer."

Vledder looked grim.

"Yes, I would like him to explain how his cigarette lighter happened to be found near the corpse of Mabel Paddington."

DeKok pursed his lips.

"I can explain that."

The young men looked at him suspiciously.

"You?" they asked in unison.

DeKok nodded slowly.

"It was a false trail, a red herring. The lighter was a plant, it was placed there *after* the murder."

Dijk swallowed. He was not as used to DeKok's methods as Vledder.

"Who?" he asked.

DeKok did not answer. Vledder groaned inwardly. DeKok was in one of his moods. Ignoring things and being unnecessarily cryptic.

But DeKok stood up and motioned for the young men to follow him. They went to the next interrogation room. DeKok paused momentarily, then he opened the door.

A slender, blonde woman leaned against the radiator in the room. She was pale, disheveled.

Vledder looked at her with incredulity. He had not expected this bomb-shell.

DeKok nodded complacently.

"Mrs. Hoveneer . . . better known as Alida Somers . . . legal spouse of Tjeerd Talema."

23

"Did she kill Mabel Paddington? When did you arrest her? Where? Who told you her name was Alida Somers? Why did Tjeerd want to kill her? Did she know . . ."

DeKok covered his ears with both hands.

"I can't answer all those questions at once," he protested. "First let's taste this wonderful cognac. It's really something special." He held his glass against the light. "Cheers . . . to the end of crime."

He had invited Vledder and Dijk for a last conference at his home. He obviously enjoyed both the company and the curiosity of his younger colleagues. He was comfortably seated in a leather chair next to the fireplace, old slippers on his feet and a venerable cognac in his hand.

Vledder shook his head sadly.

"I still don't understand it all."

DeKok laughed.

"Be easy. Until very recently I didn't understand what was happening either." He took a long, slow swallow from the cognac. "In order to put things in perspective, we should first go back to Utrecht, about three and half years ago. That was the day that Tjeerd Talema met Alida Somers for the first time. It would turn out to be a bad day for a lot of

233

people, that day in August." He placed his glass on a small table next to his chair and leaned back into the cushions. "It was one of those accidental meetings that are capable of determining people's fates and lives. Although we should not go into weighty philosophical reflections, that innocent little chat at a bus-stop in Utrecht *did* have far-reaching consequences. Alida Somers had, at the time of the meeting, an extensive criminal background. In Belgium she had been involved in a series of frauds, blackmail attempts and thefts. When the ground became too hot for her shapely feet, she came to Holland. Then, as now, it was simply a matter of walking across the border."

He took a sip from his cognac and raised an index finger into the air.

"It was uncanny," he continued, "how naively Tjeerd fell into her trap. He was completely blinded by her beauty, besotted by her body and mesmerized by what he perceived as her generous, sacrificing love for him."

Vledder looked at him in surprise.

"Did she *really* love him?"

"Who can tell. She liked him. She looked at him as a nice, uncomplicated boy, a young man with little experience. Maybe she felt something that could be compared to 'love' in the very beginning. But when her criminal mind conceived certain possibilities, whatever love was there, paled in the face of her all-consuming greed."

"What possibilities?"

DeKok grinned.

"Tjeerd had told her about picturesque, but sleepy Zoetekamp ... and about his great friend and fellow-student, Dr. Hoekstra, who had recently taken over a practice there. Alida listened carefully. She asked intelligent questions about the peculiarities of the village, the young doctor, the traditions connected with births and deaths. She also carefully researched Tjeerd's family relations. When she was convinced that her plan had a reasonable chance of success, she enticed him into a hasty marriage."

DeKok drained his glass and picked up the bottle. He poured himself another generous measure and held the bottle up with an unspoken question in his eyes. Vledder held out his glass. Dijk hastily finished the little that was left in his glass and also accepted a refill. The ritual completed, DeKok again took up the narrative.

"Tjeerd was exhilarated, he was intoxicated with happiness. His lovely bride had no trouble persuading him to agree to a wild, expensive honeymoon in exotic Saint Tropez. A trip that was far beyond his financial means. But Alida behaved as if she had married a millionaire. She would only stay in the most expensive hotels and nagged and cajoled for expensive dresses and jewelry. Within a few short weeks Tjeerd discovered that the money was gone, even his savings had been spent. He wired his boss, asked for and received a loan. In addition to the money, his boss wired a friendly, but urgent request to end the honeymoon and return to work."

"Did he go?"

"No. Alida didn't feel like going back to chilly, damp Holland. She created violent scenes and indulged in long, inconsolable bouts of crying. Tjeerd was at wit's end. He explained that the money was gone and that he had been forced to borrow from his boss. That was the moment for Alida to reveal her plans. She was sly, oh yes, extremely sly about it. The way she presented the plan it sounded so simple, so risk-free, that Tjeerd eventually agreed."

Vledder moved toward the edge of his chair.

"What sort of plan?" His voice trembled with impatience.

DeKok smiled.

"Life insurance."

Dijk looked surprised.

"Life Insurance?" he asked.

DeKok nodded.

"The young couple traveled to a number of European cities, stayed for a while and then bought life insurance policies on young and healthy Tjeerd Talema. His age, his health and his profession made him a prime target for insurance brokers everywhere. They were careful not to overdo it. The policies were for reasonable amounts and did not awaken the suspicions of the various companies. It was certainly not strange that a caring husband would get a policy to benefit his young wife. A number of companies tried to sell them more insurance than they were willing to take out. The couple was always persuaded by the sales talks."

DeKok made a grandiose gesture.

"It was almost too easy. Within months the total benefits of the policies were well over a million. With difficulty they managed to scrape together enough to pay the first few premiums. Alida, reverting back to her past lifestyle, committed some small thefts and . . . they succeeded. But time was running out."

DeKok paused and took the time to indulge in the heady aroma of his cognac. With his eyes closed he enjoyed the flavorful bouquet. DeKok was a connoisseur of cognac and these moments were important to him.

"Oh, go on, please," interrupted Mrs. DeKok. "Don't keep us in suspense."

DeKok opened his eyes and looked around at the expectant faces.

"During February of the following year," he said, "Tjeerd traveled to remote, isolated Zoetekamp . . . in order to die."

Vledder sank back in his chair.

"So, that was it," he said, relaxed but with an undertone of disappointment in his voice. "Alida Somers needed an official copy of the Death Certificate in order to collect on the policies."

Dijk frowned, stared at his glass. DeKok hastened to refill the detective's empty snifter. The movement made him look up.

"I haven't been involved from the beginning," said Dijk apologetically, "and I must say that I don't follow what you're talking about."

DeKok gave him a friendly grin.

"Say what you must, but I'll be happy to explain further. You see, Tjeerd only went to Zoetekamp to die *officially*, not literally. Dr. Hoekstra aided and abetted him thereby. The doctor signed a false Death Certificate, took care of the funeral, everything."

"Why?"

"Partly because of friendship, but also for a share of the take."

"And they succeeded?"

"Yes. They were close to being discovered when an old carpenter, who made the coffins for the village, discovered warm feet on the 'corpse' of Tjeerd. But apart from that, everything went swimmingly."

"Then what went wrong?"

DeKok shook his head sadly.

"Nothing went wrong. Alida, the sorrowing widow, suitably dressed in black, traveled from one insurance company to the next, showed the official Death Certificate and collected the money from the policies. There were no problems. But as you'll understand, Tjeerd could not show himself anywhere. At least not for a while. The couple agreed to meet on the Isle of Ibiza, in Spain, after six months. That would give Alida plenty of time to collect all the money and Tjeerd's funeral would have been more or less forgotten. They would change their names and they would live happily ever after, bolstered by an adequate income provided by the interest on the collected funds."

* * *

Dijk frowned.

"But something went wrong," he persisted.

DeKok nodded.

"Something *did* go wrong. Not with the plan, you understand, but because Alida thought herself untouchable. I mean, according to her, neither Tjeerd, nor the doctor, could touch her. They certainly couldn't take her to court. As far as she was concerned, the operation ceased as soon as she had the loot in her possession. She never went to Ibiza. She never planned to go there. Tjeerd Talema had done his duty, performed his function. He was no longer needed. It was the end of the affair, as far as she was concerned."

"What a bitch," remarked Vledder.

"Yes, a nasty woman," corrected DeKok gently.

Vledder blushed. He knew DeKok's old-fashioned concepts of language, especially in front of women. He bowed awkwardly in the direction of Mrs. DeKok. She smiled brightly. She liked Vledder and in her heart she agreed with the young man's assessment of Alida. But of course, it would never do to say that to DeKok.

"She took the money and went to Antwerp," continued DeKok, apparently unaware of the silent by-play between his wife and his assistant. "She had a lot of contacts in the underworld there, from before. Within the week she had a different identity, complete with all necessary papers and back-up material. She had become Alice de Montereau, an offspring from vaguely French nobility and she settled in Amsterdam where she was unknown. Soon, the young, beautiful *française* was a favorite guest at a number of fashionable parties. She studied her environment carefully, tested a number of marriageable candidates and within a year she had changed her name again. Alida Somers, aka Alida Talema, aka Alice de Montereau, was now Mrs. Hoveneer."

"And what about Tjeerd?"

DeKok shrugged his shoulders in a dejected manner.

"Tjeerd Talema waited on Ibiza, but his wife did not appear. At first he found it difficult to believe in her deceit. He stayed on the island in the forlorn hope that she might still turn up. In order to live, he took a job as a dishwasher."

"But he was a lawyer!"

"Yes, in Holland. In Holland he was a *dead* lawyer. In Spain he was a dishwasher. Anyway, when she still had not arrived a year after his 'official' death in Zoetekamp, he reluctantly came to the conclusion that he had been cheated, had been used. He also realized in what sort of predicament she had placed him and his friend. He was dead, he no longer existed. Even his name was gone. Several times he was on the verge of confessing all to the proper authorities, but was restrained by the thought of what would happen to his friend, Dr. Hoekstra. Slowly his feeling for Alida turned to hate . . . an all-consuming hate for the woman who had so betrayed and disillusioned him."

"He went looking for her?"

DeKok looked at Vledder.

"Yes. He left Ibiza and traveled from town to town. It will always remain a mystery how he eventually managed to find her. But we *do* know that he had plans to kill her. He was careful about that. He spied out the land, so to speak. He studied the house on the Emperor's Canal and when he discovered that Mabel wasn't part of the family, he planned an encounter with her."

Vledder smiled.

"Mabel Paddington," he said with fond remembrance in his voice. Then his face fell, thinking about how he had last seen her. "Poor thing," he sighed.

DeKok nodded agreement.

"Yes, in more ways than one. At one time, Dick, you suggested that Marcel, as we knew him then, only used Mabel's feelings for him in order to gain access to the house. You were entirely correct. He needed her and he used her."

"But why?"

"Because Mrs. Hoveneer gave him no opportunity to attack her outside the house. She took care always to be seen with others."

Vledder looked at him amazement.

"She did?"

DeKok made an impatient gesture.

"She had seen him," he declared sharply.

"What?"

"Yes. She must have discovered him early. Probably during the time he was spying on the house. You can imagine how that shocked her. She knew full well what to expect. And she couldn't warn anybody. There was nobody she could trust, unless she was willing to reveal her secret."

"Of course," interjected Dijk, who started to put the missing pieces together.

"Alida Somers, child of Antwerp's slums had come a long way. She had a large, beautiful house in one of the most prestigious neighborhoods of Amsterdam, she was rich and was married to a rich man. She had a certain standing in the community. The last thing she needed was a ghost from the past. But disaster was about to strike. One day, while driving through town with her husband, she saw Tjeerd ... arm in arm with Mabel."

"Wow," exclaimed Vledder. He took DeKok's offended glance in his stride.

"That same night," continued DeKok, "Robert Hoveneer made a scene at the dinner table. He had surprised Mabel and her boy-friend. He hid his jealousy by professing concern about strangers in the house."

Vledder nodded.

"And this alerted Mrs. Hoveneer to the fact that the danger had already penetrated beyond the walls of her own home."

"Yes and she was alerted to something else. She realized that she had somebody in the house who had a reasonable motive to kill the so-called tramp."

"Jealous Robert," said Vledder.

"But what about the murders?" asked Dijk.

DeKok did not answer at once. He lifted the bottle of venerable cognac. The large snifters were refilled once more. They all took time to savor the aroma and to enjoy the taste of the velvet liquid. Then DeKok went on.

"Alida knew that Tjeerd would come for her, sooner or later. So she made it easy for him. She used the excuse that her own room was too noisy and moved to another room, on the same floor as Robert. A room that could be easily reached from the outside via a balcony. She waited resignedly. She was counting on the fact that Tjeerd would not surprise her, kill her in her sleep, but would wake her, identify himself as the man she had cheated. That's exactly what happened. Late at night on the fourteenth, Tjeerd climbed into her room. We don't know if he still intended to kill her at that time. From the unfinished letter we learned that his hate had abated."

DeKok peered into his glass. When he continued his voice was sad.

"He never had a chance. She hit him from behind with a poker. To avoid blood spots in her room, she wrapped a towel around his head and dragged him to Robert's room. She knew Robert wasn't home yet. Her intent was clear. When the body was discovered in Robert's room, the investigation would concentrate on the presumed jealous rivalry between the two men, Robert and Tjeerd."

"Devilish," exclaimed Mrs. DeKok.

"But the corpse was found in the canal," observed Vledder.

DeKok agreed.

"But that was because of Mabel," he said. "Mabel caught Mrs. Hoveneer with the corpse."

"What!?"

"Yes, on her way to the bathroom, Mabel passed Robert's door. The door was ajar. She happened to glance inside and saw Mrs. Hoveneer leaning over the body of a man. She was in the process of removing the towel from around the bloody head. Naturally Mabel thought that something had happened to Robert and entered the room.

Horrified, she recognized her Marcel and . . . drew the wrong conclusion."

"She thought that Robert had killed him."

"Exactly. Mrs. Hoveneer was quick to reinforce the impression. She had, so she said, been awakened by a noise. When she investigated she found Robert's door open and the body of a man on the floor. Mabel admitted knowing the man. Mrs. Hoveneer countered with the suggestion that it would be terrible for Uncle Charles if Robert had to go to jail for something that he had done, although misplaced, for love of Mabel."

"Really," said Mrs. DeKok with disgust in her voice.

"Yes," agreed her husband. "Anyway," he continued, "Mrs. Hoveneer was, and is, an accomplished con-artist as we have learned. She managed to persuade Mabel to help her drop the body in the canal. The idea seemed more attractive to her than the original plan. If Mabel then kept her mouth shut, nobody would even suspect that the crime had been committed in the Hoveneer household."

"What cold-blooded calculation," said Dijk with grudging admiration. "Any normal person would have panicked. But what about Mabel? Did she keep her mouth shut?"

DeKok shook his head.

"No, she wasn't as cool as Alida. She didn't have the same presence of mind. Mabel was an artist, more emotional, more imaginative. She could not live with the thought of what had happened. A human being had been killed and that could not be nullified by tossing the body into a canal. Her nature rebelled at the thought."

DeKok took a long, slow sip from his favorite beverage. The others were used to these interruptions, or, as in the case of Inspector Dijk, were getting used to them.

"After a restless night full of doubt and despair she came to see me at the station. You know the strange, incoherent story she told me at that time. Perhaps I should have asked more penetrating questions. That's a moot point now. She was probably prompted by the realization that she was actually an accomplice to murder by having helped to remove the body. Alida made sure she understood the consequences ... afterward. Whatever the reason, she accused Robert and left it at that, offered no proof."

"But Robert was innocent," remarked Dijk superfluously.

"Right," admitted DeKok. "Robert was innocent. I wonder when she realized that she had falsely accused him. She probably came to that realization while she was hiding out in Cat's Mews. Certainly she must have started thinking after we released Robert. That's when she must have looked for motives. Motives that would induce Mrs. Hoveneer to kill an unknown tramp. Maybe Marcel, aka Tjeerd had told her certain things that took on an entirely different meaning in retrospect. But most likely she had an opportunity to go through some old papers at the Emperor's Canal."

"Papers?" asked Vledder, "I know nothing about papers."

"Yes, the original Talema-Somers Marriage Certificate and the Death Certificate from Zoetekamp. I know that Mrs. Hoveneer did not destroy them until a few days before her arrest. She had kept them. Sentimentality, perhaps. Whatever the reason, Mabel could have found out about the earlier connection between the present Mrs. Hoveneer and her Marcel. But like me, she had no proof."

"But why didn't she come to us," exclaimed Vledder vehemently. "With those hints, we could have delivered the proof. She would be alive today."

DeKok nodded soothingly.

"I told you, she was, and felt herself to be, an accomplice to murder. Perhaps she counted on clemency if we could discover the killer through information she provided." He raked his fingers through his hair. "She never got that far. Mrs. Hoveneer intervened in another life."

"You mean," asked Dijk, "that Mrs. Hoveneer killed Mabel as well?"

"That's exactly what I mean."

Dijk frowned.

"How did she know the address."

DeKok explained what he had discovered from the photographer in Utrecht.

"When I saw the pictures, I recognized Mrs. Hoveneer, I saw the connection, but I was too late to save Mabel," he added wearily.

"Well, we have everybody at this time, either dead, or in jail. What about Dr. Hoekstra? When do we pick him up?"

DeKok scratched behind his ear. He avoided looking at his young colleague.

"Never. I mean, that would be difficult."

"How's that?"

"This morning I received a telegram from him." he patted his pockets without result. "I must have lost the copy already," he confessed sheepishly. "But it came from Kenya, or Somalia, or Nigeria ... I always have trouble keeping track of those African nations." He smiled. "The doctor is well. They immediately provided him with a lot of patients."

Vledder slapped his hands down on the arm rests of his chair.

"You let him escape, of course. I should have known!"

DeKok looked at him and shook his head.

245

"Sometimes," he chided, "you say the naughtiest things."

About the Author:

Albert Cornelis Baantjer (BAANTJER) first appeared on the American literary scene in September, 1992 with "DeKok and Murder on the Menu". He was a member of the Amsterdam Municipal Police force for more than 38 years and for more than 25 years he worked Homicide out of the ancient police station at 48 Warmoes Street, on the edge of Amsterdam's Red Light District. The average tenure of an officer in "the busiest police station of Europe" is about five years. Baantjer stayed until his retirement.

His appeal in the United States has been instantaneous and praise for his work has been universal. "If there could be another Maigret-like police detective, he might well be Detective-Inspector DeKok of the Amsterdam police," according to *Bruce Cassiday* of the International Association of Crime Writers. "It's easy to understand the appeal of Amsterdam police detective DeKok," writes *Charles Solomon* of the Los Angeles Times. Baantjer has been described as "a Dutch Conan Doyle" (Publishers Weekly) and has been favorably compared to Sjöwall and Wahlöö (Kirkus Reviews).

Perhaps part of the appeal is because much of Baantjer's fiction is based on real-life (or death) situations encountered during his long police career. He writes with the authority of an expert and with the compassion of a person who has seen too much suffering. He's been there.

The critics and the public have been quick to appreciate the charm and the allure of Baantjer's work. Seven "DeKok's" have been used by the (Dutch) Reader's Digest in their series of condensed books (called "Best Books" in Holland). In his native Holland, with a population of less than 15 million people, Baantjer has sold more than 4 million books and according to the Netherlands Library Information Service, a Baantjer/DeKok is checked out of a library more than 700,000 times per year.

A sampling of American reviews suggests that Baantjer may become as popular in English as he is already in Dutch.

Murder in Amsterdam
Baantjer

The two very first "DeKok" stories for the first time in a single volume. In these stories DeKok meets Vledder, his invaluable assistant. The book contains two complete novels. In *DeKok and the Sunday Strangler*, DeKok is recalled from his vacation in the provinces and tasked to find the murderer of a prostitute. The young, "scientific" detectives are stumped. A second murder occurs, again on Sunday and under the same circumstances. No sign of a struggle, or any other kind of resistance. At the last moment DeKok is able to prevent a third murder. In *DeKok and the Corpse on Christmas Eve*, a patrolling constable notices a corpse floating in the Gentlemen's Canal. Autopsy reveals that she has been strangled and that she was pregnant. "Silent witnesses" from the purse of the murdered girl point to two men who played an important role in her life. The fiancee is suspect, but who is the second man? In order to preserve his Christmas Holiday, DeKok wants to solve the case quickly.

First American edition of these European
Best-Sellers in a single volume.

ISBN 1 881164 00 4

Some critical reviews of **Murder in Amsterdam**:

The two novellas make an irresistible case for the popularity of the Dutch author. DeKok's maverick personality certainly makes him a compassionate judge of other outsiders and an astute analyst of antisocial behavior.

> **—Marilyn Stasio, The New York Times Book Review**

This first translation of Baantjer's work into English supports the mystery writer's reputation in his native Holland as a Dutch Conan Doyle. His knowledge of esoterica rivals that of Holmes, but Baantjer wisely uses such trivia infrequently, his main interests clearly being detective work, characterization and moral complexity.

> **—Publishers Weekly**

Both stories are very easy to take.

> **—Kirkus Reviews**

DeKok and the Sorrowing Tomcat
Baantjer

Peter Geffel (Cunning Pete) had to come to a bad end. Even his Mother thought so. Still young, he dies a violent death. Somewhere in the sand dunes that help protect the low lands of the Netherlands he is found by an early jogger, a dagger protruding from his back. The local police cannot find a clue. They inform other jurisdictions via the police telex. In the normal course of events, DeKok (Homicide) receives a copy of the notification. It is the start of a new adventure for DeKok and his inseparable sidekick, Vledder. Baantjer relates the events in his usual, laconic manner and along the way he reveals unexpected insights and fascinating glimpses of the Netherlands. "The pages turn easily and DeKok's offbeat personality keeps readers interested," (Publishers Weekly).

First American edition of this European Best-Seller.

ISBN 1 881164 05 5

DeKok and the Careful Killer
Baantjer

The corpse of a young woman is found in the narrow, barely lit alley in one of the more disreputable areas of Amsterdam. She is dressed in a chinchilla coat, an expensive, leather purse is found near her right shoulder and it looks as if she died of cramps. The body is twisted and distorted. Again DeKok and his invaluable assistant, Vledder, are involved in a new mystery. There are no clues, no motives and, apparently, no perpetrators. But the young woman has been murdered. That is certain. Eventually, of course, DeKok unmasks the careful murderer, but not before the reader has taken a trip through the seamier parts of Amsterdam.

First American edition of this European Best-Seller.

ISBN 1 881164 07 1

What Others Say About Our Books
(a sampling of critical reviews provided by our readers)

About BAANTJER, the author of the "DeKok" books: The Reader's Digest has already used seven books by Baantjer in *Het Beste Boek* (Best Books), to great enjoyment of our readers (*L.C.P Rogmans,* **Editor-in-Chief, [Dutch] Reader's Digest**); A Baantjer book is checked out of a library more than 700,000 times per year (**Netherlands Library Information Service**); We have to put the second printing of his books on press before the first printing has even reached the bookstores, no matter how many we print (*Wim Hazeu,* **Baantjer's Dutch Publisher**).

MURDER IN AMSTERDAM (ISBN 1-881164-00-4) by Baantjer: If there could be another Maigret-like police detective, he might well be Detective-Inspector DeKok of the Amsterdam police. Similarities to Simenon abound in any critical judgement of Baantjer's work (*Bruce Cassiday,* **International Association of Crime Writers**); The two novellas make an irresistible case for the popularity of the Dutch author. DeKok's maverick personality certainly makes him a compassionate judge of other outsiders and an astute analyst of antisocial behavior (*Marilyn Stasio,* **The New York Times Book Review**); Both stories are very easy to take (**Kirkus Reviews**); Inspector DeKok is part Columbo, part Clouseau, part genius, and part imp. Baantjer has managed to create a figure hapless and honorable, bozoesque and brilliant, but most importantly, a body for whom the reader finds compassion (*Steven Rosen,* **West Coast Review of Books**); This first translation of Baantjer's work into English supports the mystery writer's reputation in his native Holland as a Dutch Conan Doyle. His knowledge of esoterica rivals that of Holmes, but Baantjer wisely uses such trivia infrequently, his main interests clearly being detective work, characterization and moral complexity (**Publishers Weekly**); Readers of this book will understand why the author is so popular in Holland. His DeKok is a complex, fascinating individual (*Ray Browne,* **CLUES: A Journal of Detection**).

DEKOK AND THE SOMBER NUDE (ISBN 1-881164-01-2) by Baantjer: It's easy to understand the appeal of Amsterdam police detective DeKok; he hides his intelligence behind a phlegmatic demeanor, like an old dog that lazes by the fireplace and only shows his teeth when the house is threatened (*Charles Solomon,* **Los Angeles Times**); Baantjer's laconic, rapid-fire storytelling has spun out a surprisingly complex web of mysteries (**Kirkus Reviews**).

DEKOK AND THE DEAD HARLEQUIN (ISBN 1-881164-04-7) by Baantjer: Baantjer's latest mystery finds his hero in fine form. As in Baantjer's earlier works, the issue of moral ambiguity once again plays heavily as DeKok ultimately solves the crimes (**Publishers Weekly**).

DEKOK AND THE SORROWING TOMCAT (ISBN 1-881164-05-5): The pages turn easily and DeKok's offbeat personality keeps readers interested (**Publishers Weekly**).

DEKOK AND THE DISILLUSIONED CORPSE (ISBN 1-881164-06-3): Baantjer seduces mystery lovers. "Corpse" titillates with its unique and intriguing twists on a familiar theme (*Rapport*, **The West Coast Review of Books**).

DEKOK AND MURDER ON THE MENU (ISBN 1-881164-31-4) by Baantjer: Terrific on-duty scenes and dialogue, realistic detective work and the allure of Netherlands locations (**The Book Reader**).

What others say about ELSINCK:

TENERIFE! (ISBN 1-881164-51-9) by Elsinck: A swiftly paced, hard-hitting story. Not for the squeamish. But nevertheless, a compelling read, written in the short take technique of a hard-sell TV commercial with whole scenes viewed in one- and two-second shots, and no pauses to catch the breath (*Bruce Cassiday,* **International Association of Crime Writers**); A fascinating work combining suspense and the study of a troubled mind to tell a story that compels the reader to continue reading (*Mac Rutherford,* **Lucky Books**); This first effort by Elsinck gives testimony to the popularity of his subsequent books. This contemporary thriller pulls no punches. A nail-biter, full of European suspense (**The Book Reader**); . . . A wonderful plot, well written — Strong first effort — Promising debut — A successful first effort. A find! — A well written book, holds promise for the future of this author — A first effort to make dreams come true — A jewel of a thriller! — An excellent book, gripping, suspenseful and extremely well written . . . (**A sampling of Dutch press reviews**).

MURDER BY FAX (ISBN 1-881164-52-7) by Elsinck: Elsinck has created a technical tour-de-force. This high-tech version of the epistolary novel succeeds as the faxed messages quickly prove capable of providing plot, clues and characterization (**Publishers Weekly**); This novel by Dutch author Elsinck is so interestingly written it might be read for its creative style alone. It is sharp and concise and one easily becomes involved enough to read it in one sitting. MURDER BY FAX cannot help but have its American readers fall under the spell of this highly original author (*Paulette Kozick,* **West Coast Review of Books**); This clever and breezy thriller is a fun exercise. The crafty Dutch author peppers his fictional fax copies with clues and red herrings that make you wonder who's behind the scheme. Elsinck's spirit of inventiveness keeps you guessing up to the satisfying end (*Timothy Hunter,* **[Cleveland] Plain Dealer**); The use of modern technology is nothing new, but Dutch writer Elsinck takes it one step further (*Peter Handel,* **San Francisco Chronicle**); . . . Riveting — Sustains tension and is totally believable — An original idea, well executed — Unorthodox — Engrossing and frightening — Well conceived, written and executed — Elsinck sustains his reputation as a major new writer of thrillers . . . (**A sampling of Dutch press reviews**).

CONFESSION OF A HIRED KILLER (ISBN 1-881164-53-5) by Elsinck: Elsinck saves a nice surprise, despite its wild farrago of murder and assorted intrigue (**Kirkus Reviews**); Elsinck remains a valuable asset to the thriller genre. He is original, writes in a lively style and researches his material with painstaking care (*de Volkskrant,* **Amsterdam**).

INTERCONTINENTAL PUBLISHING does not have a clipping service. These reviews come to us by courtesy of our many fans and readers of quality mystery books.